SUSAN DWORKIN

THE
COMMONS

A DIVIDED LIGHT PROJECT

OTHER BOOKS BY SUSAN DWORKIN

Desperately Seeking Susan (novelization of the film)

Double De Palma

Lost in the System (with Charlotte Lopez)

Making Tootsie

Miss America 1945

Stolen Goods, a novel

The Book of Candy, a novel

The Ms. Guide to a Woman's Health
(with Dr. Cynthia W. Cooke)

The Nazi Officer's Wife (with Edith Hahn Beer)

Weeding Out the Tears (with Jeanne White)

The Viking in the Wheat Field

ISBN-978-0-9892848-4-4

Cover design by Judy Fucci

Printed in the United States of America

FOR THE KIDS

THE COMMONS

PART ONE

IN THE LITTLE GRAY ROOM

Professor Stevie Foster did not ordinarily tell jokes. But this week had brought a great success, he was in a happy mood, and so on a snack break, he gathered together his colleagues and postdocs and all their robots and began to tell a good old joke about a chicken. He had just reached the punchline part when the ordermen burst into his lab and arrested him for treason.

A gentle Texan in his mid-60s, freckled and bald except for a fringe of faded red hair, Stevie was known for his dislike of contention and strife and did not put up a fight. But when his associates raised a great clamor of protest, and a bright white light blazed over each of them, indicating that their DNA had been identified and they were being placed on file for possible prosecution down the road, Stevie became infuriated. He lashed out at his burly captors, hurling curses. They smashed his face. His lenses dripped from his eyes. His nose broke. One of his battered old cowboy boots went flying across the lab and crashed into a tray of seedlings. The ordermen threw a hood over Stevie's head and shackled his hands.

His colleagues watched helplessly as their leader, a brilliant wheat breeder and a loveable guy, was dragged away.

Much later, when they freed his hands and pulled off the hood, Stevie found himself in a little gray room. A tall young woman crouched on the floor in a corner as far away from the toilet as possible. Her hair was wet, its ribbons and curls all ragged. Trails of tears cut across her smeared face. A fierce scarlet scar, like a fresh burn, encircled her neck. Stevie recognized her as the rising young pop star, Lizzie Corelli, lead singer of a certain band whose name he could not now recall. The glittery blue costume which she had been wearing when the ordermen captured her was ripped and stained black.

"You're bleeding," he said.

"No no no don't be alarmed, it's not my blood," she assured him.

Grunting with pain, Stevie managed to lower himself onto the floor next to her. In the several hours since his capture, violet bruises had spread across his face. His right eye had disappeared into swelling.

Lizzie had some water in a tube. She held it to his lips. She tore off a piece of his lab coat and wet it and gently dabbed at the blood drying under his nose. Knowing how badly he must be hurting, she adjusted her long body so he could lean against her.

"I remember you," she said. "You were at my great uncle's funeral. You were one of the pallbearers. "

"And I have heard you on The Beam," he said. "A concert you and your band put on at the germplasm bank in Antarctica. My colleagues and I played and replayed that concert in the lab. We learned all the words. We sang along."

Despite her filthy and disheveled condition, Stevie could see she was a lovely girl. Her curly hair, now matted and clotted with sweat and blood, and her skin were of the same warm, light brown color, and her eyes were dark blue. Even now, her eyes harbored a cheerful twinkle behind those thick dark lashes.

"Bet you anything this'll all work out in the end," she said.

"I seriously doubt that, Lizzie."

"Maybe they'll send us into exile at one of the plantations. I always wanted to see the jungle."

"We'll be lucky if we see tomorrow."

"Well, it certainly doesn't do any good to expect the worst. I believe that people should believe in a happy ending up to the absolutely last possible minute."

Stevie carefully spit a tooth into his palm.

"You don't have a helluva tight grip on reality, kid. But you sure do sing like an angel."

Even though they had both been cited as members of a vast left wing conspiracy, Professor Stevie Foster and Lizzie Corelli had never actually spoken to each other before this moment. So during their time together in the little gray room, they told each other their stories.

He told her than the man she loved was like a son to him, and that made her like a daughter in his heart.

She sang him a song about a tethered calf and a soaring swallow and the promise of freedom.

And they tried to figure out how they had come to be partners and comrades and hunted enemies of the state.

PART TWO

1. GRANDMA'S VACATION

The idea of the vacation – a gift for Grandma's 120th birthday – came up two years ago, during a meeting at the farm of my Aunt Petunia and Uncle Furlong in northern California. Mom had closed up her antique store, "The Past on Pico Two", for a whole day so we could attend. I knew it would be an important meeting because she had actually changed out of her faded blue suit with the snack stains and put on gray slacks and a clean white corn silk blouse.

All the way on the hoverbus from NewLA, she lectured me about the stupidity of me blowing my waitressing money on singing lessons and piano lessons and how was I going to make a *real* living and did I have any idea how much food and water cost in 2165? "You know what they do with songbirds in hard times, Lizzie? They eat them for breakfast!"

I did not engage. I tried to tune out. I knew Mom had been traumatized by her childhood experiences with starvation. Peanut paste, rodent stew, long lines of parched people waiting with pitcher and pail. I was sympathetic, really I was. But I had heard it and heard it and, like most of us kids, I had begun to find it – sorry, folks – kind of boring.

Mom is just under five feet tall, typical size for her generation. She wears her lenses on a red ribbon around her neck. Pulls her brown hair straight back into a pony tail, which she sometimes rolls up into a mean little bun. A thin scar runs from her forehead diagonally across her nose, just missing the inner corner of her eye, and ends on her cheekbone. From this scar you can deduce that somebody once tried to slice off Mom's face.

In the Army, she was a decorated sharp shooter. The picture that hangs near the front door of the antique store – she is young and cute and grinning, Dad is young and handsome and two feet taller than she is -- was taken on the day she received her medal.

I have never in my entire life seen her look as happy as she looks in that picture.

At the meeting in Uncle Furlong's farmhouse, Mom and I sat on one side of the table. Aunt Petunia and Uncle Furlong and their massive jock son, Odin, sat on the other side. Their daughter, Athena, attended the meeting by Incoming since she was down in Antarctica, working with Professor Bjornsdottir at the germplasm bank. She sat at the table too, but of course only virtually, stylishly cold-proofed in her quilted pink lab coat and matching ear muffs, surrounded by bags of frozen seeds.

Leave it to my cousin Theenie to look terrific under a glacier.

Even though we were both 19, Athena had finished high school two years before me. Many people think she's a genius. We're both tall. However, she is normal tall. Like 5'4". And I am 5'11"(!) A genetic gift from my dead father and his Masai ancestors. I can hardly ever find any nice clothes in my size. Thanks a lot, fellas.

Aunt Petunia kicked off the proceedings.

"Since our family is fortunate enough to have that rare treasure, an actual living grandparent," she announced, "my dear Furlong thinks we should give Grandma a nice present for her forthcoming 120th birthday."

Athena suggested a diamond brooch.

Aunt Petunia fretted about which of us kids would inherit it.

Odin suggested a big party. "

"It'll be a mob scene!" Petunia protested. "All those waiters and waitresses who used to work for Grandma in her restaurant, all those ex-lovers..."

"How's about a vacation?" Mom suggested.

"Maybe a spa," Uncle Furlong said.

"Sounds perfect," Athena added. "Someplace where Grandma can soak in whirly pools like she likes to do and have massages and sit in hot places, and then sit in cold places and be slathered with elixirs."

"My Incoming has told me about resorts up north where the gladiators go to do that kind of thing," Odin said. "Fancy places with lots of water."

Uncle Furlong exclaimed: "Good thinking!" and slammed Odin on his brawny back. Odin looked pleased. Thinking is not his customary gift. He usually does nothing but develop his ginormous muscles and play soccer. (Grandma once told me that there used to be another kind of soccer called football. After the famine and the food wars and the revolution and the restoration of order, when the Corporation became the government, it was outlawed because it caused brain damage in young men, and we couldn't afford to lose any more of them.)

Clearly, Aunt Petunia did not like the direction of the conversation.   Her long nose lengthened. Her narrow eyes narrowed. "And what if Grandma drinks too much at this fancy resort," she said, "and starts leading the crowd in a medley of oldies and some enterprising gladiator falls in love with her and gets her to marry him, thus compromising our clan estate? What if she slips in the sweatsy room and breaks one of those fancy new bones of hers?" She smiled and finally laid on us her true objective. "I say we have a nice birthday dinner at home. I'll bake a cake. With real chicken eggs."

"I kind of liked the spa idea," Odin said.

"Me too," said Uncle Furlong.

"Me too," said Athena.

Aunt Petunia glared at them. I had the feeling they would all feel her wrath later on.

Mom said: "But Petunia clearly has a point about the dangers of letting Grandma take such a trip by herself. Obviously someone must go along with her."

I was sitting quietly by a window, pretending not to have heard a word of the "Grandma's vacation" conversation, gazing out at the hoverreapers drifting over the wheat, harvesting, separating, milling it into flour and packing it into sacks right there in the fields. I was thinking how beautiful agriculture is and how profitable, and how much better my relationship with Mom would be if only I would give up music and go to work on Uncle Furlong's farm.

"What do you say, Lizzie?" asked Mom.

"Hmmm...uh...what?"

"Would you be willing to spend part of your summer vacation with Grandma?"

"Excuse me?"

"Up north. For two weeks. At a spa. With Grandma."

"What?! Alone with Grandma?!"

"Furlong and Petunia and I are working."

"And I have to be at training camp," Odin said.

"And I'm here in this freezing vault all alone sorting ancient grains of rice," Athena added in her most appealing little whimper. A male hand reached across her shoulder (black hairs on each knuckle) and offered her a steaming cup. She took it and looked up at the off-Incoming guy who was attached to the hand and waggled her lashes and smiled and said, without even glancing at me: "I guess that leaves you, Lizzie."

I sighed. Wrinkled my nose. Let go a long, put-upon groan "Oh gee, come on, folks, I mean what a drag! A spa?! Do I have to? There won't be any other kids. It'll all be gladiators and old people eating restricted diets and Grandma will lecture me day and night about skin care or whatever. Besides, my Incoming has told me that I'm being reviewed by the Music Talent Auction this summer. How can I not be home when the selectors announce their decision?"

"We know it's a big sacrifice," Uncle Furlong said.

"You'd be doing us all a big favor," Odin said.

"Be a sport, Lizzie," Athena said.

"Ohhhh wellll...ohhhh-kay, I'll do it," I said, very reluctantly, while thinking *A spa vacation! With Grandma! Yayyyy!* "But you guys are going to owe me big for this one."

Grandma irritates Mom because she is self-involved and absolutely gorgeous and has spent her whole life staying that way.

When she was 14, she took all the money that she had earned from baby sitting and gave it to an alchemist who developed a set of elixirs especially for her personal chemistry. When she was 16, she took all the money she had earned modeling eyelashes (Grandma holds the continental record for natural eyelash length) and spent it on a nose job and singing lessons. The years after that – the years of terrible weather and perpetual famine -- are somehow totally vague in her memory. All we know is that by the time she married Grandpa Arnie at the age of 32, she was appearing regularly on the old public web, singing jingles about products nobody remembers.

We have a clip on our clandisc of Grandpa Arnie (Uncle Furlong's father) making a toast to Grandma at their wedding, in which he says that he is the most fortunate of men to have won the heart of the most beautiful woman in North America. This was, of course, way back in the old days when there were almost nine billion people in the world instead of just fourish, and North America had three separate big countries in it. So even if you allow for the madness of love, Grandma must have been pretty pretty when she was 32.

She has not allowed herself to change since then. Her bobbed hair is still mahogany red, her skin still creamy pale and smooth. She still dresses like a media star. In chic shops all across the continent, she has special salespeople, often called Ceil, who hunt clothes for her and notify her whenever something terrific is available.

Twenty years ago, when she was 100, Grandma embarked upon a campaign of reinvention surgery that made her look younger than Mom and Aunt Petunia, and wiped out her savings. "It was," she says, "worth every penny."

Grandma came from a landless clan and was lucky enough to marry into farming. Grandpa Arnie Burton had inherited a 500-acre spread in western New Jersey. Dairy cows. During the famine, he delivered food to the starving. People wrestled over sacks of grain. Somebody started shooting. Somebody shot Arnie.

So then, just as the revolution times began, Grandma became a widow, with a little boy named Furlong, and a big career as a jingle singer, and 500 acres. Her second husband, Eddie Bright, wanted no part of it. Since The Law of All Nations says you can't share into a farm without living and working on it, Grandma sold out to the Corporation. She saved her 15% of the sale price for Uncle Furlong's future. When he grew up, he bought a farm with it.

This guy Eddie Bright, Grandma's second husband, was Mom's father. Therefore, he was my grandfather. However, I had never met him.

Mom told me that he had a very famous older brother named Dr. Clyde Bright who had done something amazing for wheat and received all kinds of medals and honors.

She said that Eddie too had been famous in his day, as a weatherman on the old public web. People trusted him. They called him "Eddie Bright, the Farmer's Friend." Every storm he predicted happened.

But then, during the food wars, when all able-bodied shareholders (including my Mom and Dad) were fighting to keep the raiders away from our granaries, Eddie went crazy in the middle of the weather report and attacked the Corporation for hoarding stocks of wheat to keep the supply low and the price high and causing people and animals around the world to starve, which set off the wars that were currently raging.

Uncle Furlong said it was stupid thing for Eddie to do.

I thought it was brave.

Rather than stick around and wait to be punished for sedition or rebellion or whatever, Eddie took off and went into permanent hiding. He was now officially classified as a fugitive from justice

Occasionally he would put out some copies of an illegal newsletter (on paper!) attacking the Corporation or the Chinese Empire or the Caliph of the New Ottoman Orbit. He would drop the newsletters from the wings of swallows. They were immediately scooped up, not so much because of their politics – because nobody really thought anybody could overthrow the

Corporation or the Empire or the Caliph – but because they also contained the most accurate weather report available anywhere.

The newsletters would disappear into people's socks and underwear. They were burned. Or eaten. (I have always found that amazing about paper, I mean, how it can be made to vanish.) Although nobody would admit to having read the newsletters, all the agroclans waited impatiently for another issue to drop out of the sky so they could know when the next hurricane was going to make landfall.

Grandpa Eddie abandoned his money when he became a fugitive. The Corporation gave Grandma her 15% share in the divorce. She decided that because she had lost two husbands in New Jersey, it was not a lucky place for her. She kept both their names as a token of her affection (she is called Foxie Burton Bright) and moved west to NewLA. Then she used Eddie's money to open her famous restaurant – "Foxie's, Where Dinner Comes A'Singing."

Grandma promised that someday she would tell me the whole story of how she met Eddie Bright.

She would get a longing look on her face when somebody mentioned him, as though she missed him.

I wondered whether he missed her. And Mom. And me.

I wondered whether he maybe thought about us sometimes.

I know it wasn't fair that I was Grandma's favorite grandchild. It just happened. Genetic serendipity.

For starters, neither Athena nor Odin wanted to listen to Grandma's stories. And I loved them. I loved to hear about the days before the Texas Secession; when Florida and Louisiana and OldLA were still above water; and meat wasn't made in the lab; and people only lived to be 85 or 90; when they were called "citizens" instead of "shareholders" and could eat three full meals a day instead of one plus three snacks; when farmers weren't richer than everybody else. Amazing times.

Grandma loved that I loved her stories.

In addition, I was the only grandchild who, like Grandma, could sing. At an early age, Grandma declared that I actually sang much better than she did and that, if I received the proper training, I would one day be a Beamstar.

Mom couldn't have disagreed more. "Why are you filling her head with impossible dreams?! Stop trying to design her future, you narcissistic meddler! Leave my little girl alone."

But truth be told, Grandma was right, and we all knew it. I had this big round bluesy voice and perfect pitch. I could hear the piccolos go one tone off key in a Mahler symphony. I could hear the thunder before anybody else knew it was going to rain. I never got the lead in school musicals, because I made the other kids look like specks in the distance. But as soon as I graduated, I began to get professional gigs. I would sing "The Farmer is a Friend to All" at virtual agroclan meetings. I did several live weddings and even some funerals, and that gave me a bit of experience looking into the actual faces of the people in the audience. Usually I would sing songs that the hosts had rented already. However, if they left the selection up to me, I would always pick songs that were more than 250 years old, because these didn't have to be rented from the Corporation.

Grandma told me that the lyrics and titles and tunes of popular songs had changed since she was a girl. They were basically the same songs, she said, but different. Mutated, or somehow reconstituted, like the peachies that used to be called peaches and the cukettes that used to be called cucumbers. The songs that didn't change tended to be the ancient ones, because they could be had for free and people used them all the time and never forgot them.

Grandma felt it wasn't fair that she had to pay the Corporation for every song under 250 years old that was sung at her restaurant.

"After a couple of generations, music should belong to the commons," she would say.

"Who's that?" I would ask.

"Us," she would say. "All of us."

In Grandma's day, young people like me and my cousins Athena and Odin used to have to pay to go to college. It wasn't like now, when you're selected at one of the auctions – for Music, Math, Sports, whatever – and you get college and all the grad school they think you need, totally free. Athena had already aced the Agrotech auction. Odin would soon join the gladiators. My dream was to be bought by the Bloomington Music School. I'd study theory and breathing, I'd learn French, Turkish, Mandarin and add another octave to my range, and then I'd be bought by The Beam, and I'd get all the beautiful clothes I wanted, specially made in my size, and I'd sing jingles.

That was my dream. Jingles.

Mom would insist that I had to learn snack distribution, hoverbus conducting, accounting, something that would support me in case of disaster. And again it would start. Hunger would stalk the land. Dams would collapse. All the men would die.

I would run away and escape to Grandma's restaurant.

If the night was clear, we would sit together outside. She would teach me ancient songs.

Once we saw this amazing shower of explosions as the abandoned satellites swooped into earth's atmosphere and burned up.

"When I think of how much money we paid for that stuff..." Grandma muttered.

"Why did they stop working?"

"Most were blown up during the food wars. Those that remain have just died from neglect. A lot of big things that we used to depend on have been neglected to death. Because, somehow, when the weather was attacking us, big things didn't seem to be doing us much good any more. They just crashed and crumbled, and all we had left was rubble. The old governments sent robot rockets into space to look for another star where we could maybe start over, but they came up empty. We realized that this one planet was all we had. So we gave up on big things like robot rockets and nuclear reactors and satellites, and we began to sort of tiptoe over the earth. No more digging, blasting, drilling. The new governments invested in little things. Like chips and discs and genes and batteries and lenses and snacks and seeds and farms that are 2000 acres max. Because they could control those things and maintain them more easily.

"Remember that, Lizzie. Maintenance is the key to life."

When the restaurant staff had gone home and we were alone, Grandma and I would often sit down beside each other on the piano bench, hip to hip, and we would sing duets, switching off melody and harmony.

It's so much fun, such a comfort, to know that you are really good at something, that you come by it naturally as a gift from your ancestors, that it makes people happy and is just absolutely yours.

I loved to sing with Grandma. Those were my joyfullest times.

Once our clan had registered its intent to buy the vacation, promotions for the great spas of the north began to flash constantly on Mom's Incoming. She said they looked wonderful.

"The Redwood Wrestlers' Rest and Retreat", a favorite of gladiators, had three gyms and four fight stadia and a sunlift that could take you up to the top of both redwoods for a panoramic view. (Grandma swore that there used to be a whole forest of these ginormous trees, but she often exaggerates just to make the story better.)

"The New Ashland Wet Spot", built on the ruins of some wooden theatres, was just downstream from an actual river where you could go canoeing on white foaming bubbles and observe real fish swimming!

"Rose'n'Harry's", on White Bear Pond in Minnesota, specialized in VIPs. Corporate executives who had to be rewarded. Beamstars and gladiator champions and foreign dignitaries who had to be impressed. "Rose'n'Harry's" had special permission from the Chairman of the Board to serve real food.

On Grandma's actual birthday, May 8, Mom received authorization to make out-discs of all the promotions, with thrilling surround-around interactives of forests and rivers. I took them over to "Foxie's, Where Dinner Comes A'Singing" to show Grandma and let her choose where she wanted to go.

She was busy holding auditions. So I sat down in the back of the restaurant to wait and watch.

I ought to explain that "Foxie's, Where Dinner Comes A'Singing" was a nostalgia den, filled with antiques from Broadway-era live musical shows. Of course, this era ended when New York flooded, but many of the artifacts remained, and Mom said they had become quite collectible.

Old footage of actors in action streamed continuously around the lobby walls. Some tables had ancient theatre seats around them, with these formerly-famous puppets sitting on them like dinner guests. They would sing any show tune you wanted if you deposited the rental fee and pressed on their belly buttons.

Recently, Grandma had installed an interactive performance system. You could see famous dead people up there on the stage, performing as though they were actually present. If you called out a request, they would turn to you and say "This one's for..." and you'd say "Lizzie from NewLA!" And then Mr. Harburg would sing "The Rainbow Song" or Miss Warwick would sing "What I Wish for You", dedicated to you.

And if you asked a question of these great artists of yesteryear - like When did you write that? or Where did you get that wowsy great dress? - they would give you an historically accurate answer. They would autograph your napkin, shake your hand, you could even sing with them, I mean like actually get up there on stage with them and sing. And my Grandma Foxie would send you home with a disc to show everybody: you were in show business; you are no longer an orphan in history; you have a link to the past.

While the waiters served you dinner at "Foxie's", they performed musical numbers from the shows that Grandma had gone to see when she was a little girl.

Imagine this. Your waitress is Giulietta. She brings your soup, then races up on stage and, with Grandma accompanying her, she belts out, for example, a song about little girls. Then amid wild applause, Giulietta races back to your table and clears the soup bowls and serves the chicken. She's excited, breathless, even a little sweaty. And unlike the chicken, which never breathed at all, she is *real*, actually living and singing and serving right in front of you, and you get her performance, and those of all Foxie's other talented waiters and waitresses, for absolutely no extra cost with your meal.

When I asked Grandma what gave her this wonderful idea, she answered: "In life, my darling, as in art, one must always have a gimmick."

I watched her as she put the auditioners through their paces. Quietly she asked each performer: *what song? what key? what tempo? any particular style?* Whatever they wanted, Grandma provided.

A handsome old guy stepped up to sing a song about getting married in Padua, wherever that is. He gazed passionately at Grandma while he sang.

"More vibrato, Mr. Bellsworth," she said. "Yes yes that's right, lovely absolutely lovely, you're hired."

He kissed her hand.

I thought: *Someday I have to learn how to have my hand kissed.*

A bouncy brunette, with big bangs and a low, melting voice, and wearing almost nothing, said "Lola Wants B-flat." I thought she was referring to somebody named Lola who had made a special request, but it turned out that Lola was the subject of her song. (Actually, it was more like a dance.) Grandma stopped her 130 seconds in and said "Thank you. Next." The girl burst into tears and ran out of the restaurant.

A brother-sister act sang a cute song called "Friendsies" and did a soft shoe dance. Grandma hired them on the spot.

Then Paco El Din strode onto the stage.

Oh God.

He was taller than I am. He wore dusty jeans and work boots. He had green eyes and dark curly hair *and dimples!* A triangle of dark curly hair showed at the neck of his shirt. He said he was 21 years old and that he could play the piano and just about anything with strings – violin, bass, banjo, guitar, mandolin, p'i p'a, oud, harp, you name it.

"Let's hear 'Let In the Clowns' in E-minor on the violin," Grandma said. And Paco played it. "Let's hear 'Ballyhoh" in B-flat on the guitar." He played that too. "How's about 'A Little Night Music?'" she said, sliding off the piano bench. Paco took her place, laid his long fingers on the keys and played Mozart so beautifully that the cook came out of the kitchen to listen.

"Lizzie darling, go up there and sing 'Drink To Me Only With Thine Eyes'. Mr. El Din, please accompany my granddaughter."

It was a trick assignment. That song is about 500 years old. Grandma was betting this Paco prodigy guy wouldn't have any idea how to play it. But he did. He asked me for a key and I said G and we made that old sweet song together as though it had belonged to us just forever.

When it was over, everybody in the place burst into applause. Grandma was beaming. Paco and I took a little bow. He kissed my hand.

Turns out it is very easy to have your hand kissed.

The cook made Grandma a special plummish pie for her birthday and gave her a wonderful present: a little songbird named Shankar. Rosy red, fluffy feathers, teensy green eyes. Shankar immediately adored Grandma. The minute he saw her, he began to hop around inside his cage and tweet ragas.

Grandma clapped her hands and kissed the cook. She invited Paco to stay after all the other auditioners had left and join us for a piece of the scrumptious pie.

"Who are you?" she asked Paco. "Where are you from?"

"North Carolina," he answered. "Our family has 2000 acres of corn there."

"Wow!" Grandma and I said. Two thousand acres is the maximum amount of land any family can farm in North America. So this Paco El Din came from a superrich agroclan.

"Trouble is, Mama and Daddy want for me to take over the farm," he explained sadly. "And all I want to do is play music. We fight. I try loving the corn. I fail. We fight. Mama cries. She fights with Daddy. This Sunday past, we had such a big fight that Daddy threw all my strings out the front door and said 'Git!'. So I headed west, and played in bars to earn me some money to eat and to buy my next hoverbus fare.

"Man named Eddie Bright heard me playing one night. He said he was looking for a guitar player to give to the woman he loved as a birthday present. And he paid the rest of my way to NewLA.

"So here I am, Mrs. Burton Bright. I'm signed on to accompany you and your talented granddaughter whenever you want me. Happy Birthday."

Grandma began to cry.

2. **WACO IN MONGOLIA**

H ow could young Lizzie Corelli have been expected to understand her Great Uncle Clyde Bright's fame as a plant scientist and his vast contributions to her well-being?

She had never gone hungry. Almost all the plants and animals she knew had been genetically rebuilt and transformed by the time she was born. She had never seen the old nature except in pictures and therefore didn't miss it. Meteorological upheaval, famine, epidemic, political revolution and then war, all of that was just dumb history to her. She had never watched the fish being boiled alive in their own ocean. Had never encountered the red rust demon that wiped out the wheat harvest year after year after year and started the whole world spinning toward starvation.

Wheat rust had plagued humanity since the time of the Romans. No grain-growing nation had escaped its savagery. And Lizzie's Great Uncle Clyde Bright was the man who had beaten it.

In 110 years of patient, brilliant science, he had taught each of the 30 wheat varieties authorized for growing in North America to resist rust. Foreign powers had bought and stolen his work, copied it, improved on it, and now all wheat everywhere was immune. The ancient plague of rust had disappeared, extinct as bananas and tuna.

Clyde Bright's greatest students, known as The Grain Guardians, were now training other students, seeding them into the universities and the Corporation labs, protecting the magic wheat that was still, after all these centuries, called "the staff of life."

Foremost among the Grain Guardians was Professor Stevie Foster.

Stevie had come to study with Clyde Bright in Minnesota as part of the "Texas Brain Drain."

It wasn't that he felt disloyal to the secessionist republic. Quite the contrary; he ached for home. However, most of his family and all their cattle had suffocated in the dust storms and the droughts there. He had survived but in desperate poverty. His old lab was shut down. He lived in a shelter. Worked as a pyre-maker for the poor dead steers. Ate whenever he could. Washed himself not with water, which had to be saved for drinking, but with sand. Dreamed of plump girls.

An acknowledged prodigy, he could see that in desperate, starving Texas, he would never work as a scientist again. And Dr. Bright offered him not only work but glory.

Stevie had secured his place in history by successfully breeding wheat for windy places, which exactly described the fields of Lizzie's Uncle Furlong in the hills above the great valley.

Back in the 20th century, the valley had burst with fruits and vegetables, irrigated lavishly with tons of cheap, clean water. Now the water was gone. The valley and others like it across the whole southwestern quadrant had dried up. Miles of California orchards and row crops, lost; miles of Texas range, naked of forage; Tucson, Albuquerque and half of Mexico, abandoned.

Somehow, farmers had to learn to plant at higher elevations further north, where formerly freezing weather had turned temperate, and where it still regularly rained.

The problem was the wind. Every season, the thin, stony dirt on the hillsides just blew away.

'What we need," said Stevie's beloved teacher, Dr. Bright, "is a tough, tasty wheat that will grow thick matting roots to spread wide and anchor the hillsides. You've got to invent that wheat, Stevie. That's your challenge in life."

"Maybe we could try for a perennial habit," Stevie said eagerly, "so the grain could maybe blossom again by itself, and the farmers hereabouts wouldn't need to buy new seeds every year."

"Try that and they'll disappear you, my boy. This is not desperate starving Texas where you grow anything you can any way you can. Here, saving seeds for a second harvest is a capital offense. All our seed is owned by the Corporation. It has to be bought new every single year. There's hardly a weed by the wayside that still grows for free.

"Forget perennial. Just concentrate on thick matting roots. Pick the brains of Felicity Bjornsdottir over in the Seed Banking Department. Get her to dig around in the vaults and find you wild and ancient wheat varieties that used to grow at high altitudes, in freezing temps and rocky soil. Isolate the genes that enabled them to do that and breed those genes into a modern wheat and cross breed it with a tough, deep-rooted prairie grass, the kind the ancients used to build sod houses. Maybe then you will have a crop that can beat the wind."

After three years working dawn to dark in the crags of Idaho, then five more at Clyde Bright's experimental farm in Minnesota, after two wives had become fed up with his obsessive workaholic lifestyle and left him, Stevie Foster beat the wind.

In a tiny item on the New Crop Bulletin, delivered exclusively to the Incomings of selected agrotechs, he announced the development of two new wheat-rye hybrids, Galveston and Abilene.

An ambitious young Corporation head hunter named Horatio Jedda contacted him within minutes.

Horatio was a man of the war generation. Like Lizzie's parents, he had spent his youth and strength defending the Pacific coast. He came from one of the New Islands, which had risen roaring from the water during the same apocalyptic volcanic upheaval that had destroyed so much of Hawaii.

People who encountered Horatio could hardly describe what he looked like, for he had no distinguishing physical features. Height: medium. Complexion: grayish. Eyes, maybe greenish; it was hard to tell because he wore tinted lenses and never looked at anyone directly. His thick hair was cut very short. It wasn't gray exactly, but rather translucent, the color present but absent, like his drifting gaze, indeed, like his whole persona. With a voice perpetually rasping, he spoke so quietly that you had to stop whatever you were doing and concentrate all your attention to hear what he was saying.

No one could recall ever having seen Horatio Jedda smile. In fact, no one could recall ever having seen any expression on his face at all.

Like all Corporation personnel, he wore his Incoming on the back of his left hand, where it had been surgically embedded.

When he first met Stevie Foster, Jedda was just beginning to transform human resources – often considered a mere support service – into the engine that would build the Agrotech Division into the most powerful branch of the Corporation. He believed that in a depleted world, the only resource left in any abundance was the one that had done the depleting, namely people. His systems of scouts and talent auctions, percentages and pay-offs, deals that captured the best and the brightest, giving what he called "the talent" a satisfying piece of the treasure they produced, all of these would be copied by other divisions and foreign competitors too.

He took Stevie for an unforgettable meal at "Rose'n'Harry's" on White Bear Pond in Minnesota. Over the real juicy sirloin steak, he said: "Now then, Professor Foster, what do you need for your wheat breeding program? Will $200 million cover it? Three hundred hillside acres in South Dakota? Sure. We can do that."

Jedda extended his left arm. From the screen embedded on the back of his hand rose a full-scale presentation to illustrate his promises. "This is the lab we can offer you." The lab surrounded Stevie, a scientific wonderland brimming with state-of-the-art equipment. "Note our newest genome sequencer. It will complete up to 40 in less than ten minutes." Stevie gasped. "And you can select your grad students and postdocs, we'll pay their tuition, housing, per diems. Feel free to get the best." Stevie began making a mental list of the great kids he had taught. "Now then. How about a nice house in historic Deadwood?" The lab evaporated, replaced by a spacious, free-standing home with exposed ceiling beams that looked like they might be real wood. "An indoor lap pool, cleaning crew, roof gardens where you'll be able to access your own vegetables, year round," Horatio was saying. "And this lovely young lady here is Reilly Vietta, otherwise known as Miss Copper Canyon. She will be showing you around town." The luscious beauty queen smiled and beckoned to Stevie, as though she were about to take him on a tour of the house. Fooled for a moment into imagining she was really there, he reached out to take her hand. "I think you'll find her very good company," Horatio said, as she faded away.

"Once we go into production with Galveston and Abilene," he continued "you're guaranteed a royalty of 15% of the net on every seed sold. Just tap the screen. Go ahead. I assure you it will not hurt me. Tap the screen, Professor, and you're set for life."

Stevie hesitated.

"I'd kinda like to give some of the seed to foreign colleagues for research purposes," he said.

"That is an excellent idea," Horatio answered. "When you're all finished with your work and the seed is multiplied, packaged and ready to be shipped, we'll see about getting authorization to sell some overseas."

"No no, I'm not making myself clear, Mr. Jedda."

"Dr. Jedda."

"This is for scientists – for research – for breeding purposes – in other mountainous areas – South America, north central Asia, western Africa. Back in my old lab in Dallas, whenever we found a useful trait, like say drought resistance, we'd share some of the germplasm with colleagues, so they could breed the trait into their local crops. It's a tradition. Common scientific practice."

"Sharing hasn't been common scientific practice since the Corporation became the government and the people became shareholders, Professor. Please tap the screen right here." Stevie hesitated, then sighed and tapped the little screen, simultaneously guaranteeing his future and sealing his fate. "Now then. What would you like for dessert? I recommend Rose's cheese cake."

Six months later, eating his heart out in the beautiful Deadwood house, haranguing Miss Copper Canyon with litanies of guilt, longing for a colleague who would understand his situation and forgive him for not sharing his discovery, Stevie called his old friend from the Seed Banking Department, the Grain Guardian, Felicity Bjornsdottir.

She couldn't be reached.

The third Grain Guardian, Itamar Mugombo at The Sun Project, responded; but he was skittish. "Apparently you said something about sharing with foreign colleagues, my dear Stevie, and that got you put on a Corporate watch list. Now anybody who talks to you automatically falls under surveillance. One wrong remark could bring big trouble. As you know, I always try to avoid that. So goodbye."

"Wait up. Wait. Where's Felicity?"

"She felt…uh…unwell and has been sent somewhere for a rest."

"Talk plain, Itamar. What happened?"

"Bit of a breakdown."

"Felicity? No way. She's gotta be the sanest person I know!"

"Apparently not anymore." Itamar cleared his throat. "Stevie. Please. Listen. This man Jedda, he may look like a blank page, but he is increasingly important."

"What's he a doctor of?"

"History. He wrote his dissertation on Chinese agricultural policy in the late 20th century. Don't cross him. Don't bait him. Just enjoy your success and keep your mouth shut."

Stevie took Itamar's advice.

Eventually his name came off the Corporate watch list. Galveston and Abilene, like every other plant on the North American continent, became the possession of the Corporation.

Lizzie's Aunt Petunia, as president of the Ladies Auxiliary of The Northern California Agroclans Society, was given a supply to distribute among the hillside farmers, to see if the seed would anchor the soil and defend it against the wind. And it did.

The success of the new varieties dazzled the farmers. The flimsy soil began to thicken and enrich itself. Flowers sprang up along with weeds and bushes never before seen this high. Birds chattered excitedly to each other about the new cornucopia of bugs. Stevie Foster was able to send money home to his mother and his surviving brother. Lizzie's Uncle Furlong bought diamonds for her Aunt Petunia. In time, the Burton Bright agroclan grew wealthy enough to send Lizzie and her Grandma Foxie on their grand spa vacation.

For a dozen years, Stevie Foster worked diligently in his South Dakota fields, churning out useful discoveries. Horatio Jedda visited periodically — as he did with all the talent -- to check on Stevie's work, his needs, his state of mind.

Stevie was afraid of Horatio. He knew that since their first meeting, the expressionless bureaucrat had risen to great authority in the Corporation. He was rumored to have some sort of spy system that did personal work for him alone. And he had become famous in agrotech circles by securing for the Corporation sole ownership of The Antarctic Germplasm Bank.

Once an international public facility, into which every nation routinely deposited its agricultural seeds, the bank had fallen into mortal disrepair during the wars that preceded The Era of Restored Order. Collapsing governments, disintegrated bureaucracies, ruined machinery had left the precious seeds untended in the defrosting dark.

At a routine operations meeting, Horatio suggested that the Corporation could probably buy the bank for a song.

The Chairman, then newly-elected, thought for a moment and said "Do it."

And so he had. In one stroke, Horatio Jedda had privatized the essential germplasm of global agriculture. If you wanted a seed now, to improve or invent a plant, you had to apply to the

Corporation. And once approved, you had to pay. In common Corporate parlance, this was called "The Jedda Bonanza." It had helped to make the Chairman more powerful than any Chairman in memory.

No one except political insiders like Horatio ever met the Chairman. He had been elected by a secret vote of the Board for a term of ten years and had already served nine of them. A charming fellow of 125, with a bit of a belly and a bushy moustache, he was a public relations whiz. He had come to power in the unsteady years when the Fifteen Percent Deal had not quite taken hold, and North America was still rocked by little rebellions demanding more than 15% and greater control of the remaining 85%.

The Chairman had helped to settle these disputes by rigidly reorganizing the dissemination of information.

It was the Chairman who had developed the concept of the "pertinent listener", making sure that shareholders received news only on a "need to know" basis. Announcements arrived gently, on your most personal surfaces – bathroom mirror, bedroom pillow, the Incoming sealed around your wrist. Face-to-face gatherings had been replaced virtually, by "Incoming Assemblies." Those too were strictly limited in size. There were no movie screens around which large groups of shareholders might gather, no live theatre to consolidate and focus public emotions. Only the very old remembered the press.

No mass audience existed at all any more, except for the Chairman's own brief weekly message and of course Arliss' weather report.

When the Chairman became Chairman, he ushered in the ten PM cutoff for publicly performed music and the 250-year program for song rentals. He mandated that Corporate executives, including himself, should never make public appearances, explaining that this would avoid celebrity and the attendant dangers of personality cults.

As a result, the shareholders now experienced the Corporation not as a government led by individuals but as an aggregate entity, humanized but not human. No one to idolize. No one to blame.

The Board met once a month at the Chairman's large, comfortable, free-standing home in an undisclosed location. The heads of the various divisions made their reports. Realizing that Horatio Jedda was one of the few whose vision extended beyond his own administrative bailiwick, the Chairman encouraged all Board members to study his explication of Corporate operating philosophy, known as "The Sufficiency Memo."

"We live in a civilization of scarcity," Horatio wrote. *"And in a civilization of scarcity, society will only remain stable if a strict idea of 'sufficiency' is observed. No one gets too rich. Crowds and farms and towns don't get too big. No one remains a sports champion for too long. Collaborations are brief. Justice is meted out miscreant by miscreant, in private. No mass public executions as in days now thankfully gone by. Food, water, space, energy - all are strictly rationed. And every trace, every cell and seed and surviving crumb of the old nature is preserved and tended to with the utmost care, in the hope that the old future will someday return and humanity will experience abundance once again."*

Stevie knew that Horatio Jedda could eliminate his lab, his house, his generous food and water and energy allotments, and his payments to the family back in Texas with a couple of taps on the back of his left hand. For days before every meeting, he lay sleepless with anxiety, He gnawed his knuckles. His freckled, sensitive skin itched with nervous irritations.

Horatio encouraged Stevie's fear. He isolated the sensitive Texan, positioning him far away from the comfort of his friends, the other Grain Guardians, Felicity and Itamar. Keep great minds separate, and they could become competitors, the best case scenario for the Corporation. Throw them together and they could turn into collaborators, spawning dangerous ideas. Like: *We should write this in code so that only we understand.* Or worse: We *should NOT write this in code so that everybody understands.*

In the year 2164, Horatio came away from a visit to Deadwood with the distinct impression that his prize wheat breeder was growing a bit bored. He suggested, at a meeting with the International Affairs Division, that Stevie Foster might enjoy a change of scenery and a tough new challenge.

The diplomats had an idea.

Although The Tripartite Peace Treaty of 2140 had outlawed shooting wars among the three great powers, economic warfare, especially agricultural and industrial espionage, continued unabated. The Caliph of the New Ottoman Orbit maintained armies of thieves, mostly from his European and African provinces, to infiltrate North American and Chinese tech projects. The Chinese Emperor preferred robotic larceny and had begun setting up a phalanx of underground Beam readers on the northern border of Mongolia, programmed to overhear every Incoming communication from China's rivals.

The Mongols weren't happy about this, but how could they refuse? They had endured waves of starvation since flooding from melting glaciers had swamped the grazing lands of the steppes. They needed food – and the Chinese supplied them with millions of tons of wheat and rice every year.

It would be wonderful, suggested the International Affairs Division, if the Corporation could help the poor Mongols escape this stranglehold, perhaps by teaching them to breed and grow their own wind-resistant, flood-resistant, bug-resistant wheat.

In short order, Stevie Foster was riding a sunflight to The University of the Wind in Ulan Bator.

Stevie's students fanned out across the frigid foothills. They were checking on the new wheat, called Waco, which they had planted the previous autumn. The university administration, gathered in the warm Agrotech Department offices, sipped sweet steaming tea and watched the kids on their Incoming screens.

It was May 8, 2165. Foxie Burton Bright's 120th birthday. The day her granddaughter Lizzie attended auditions at her restaurant and met Paco El Din.

Stevie himself paced at the back of the room, kneading the brim of his hat with jittery fingers.

Had his Waco wintered over? Was it growing? Was it strong? Never before had wheat flourished in this terrain, at this height, subject to these fierce winds. Six simulated harvests in the lab had failed before the seventh succeeded, encouraging Stevie to try planting a crop in the field. Would this be another failure — or the moment of his greatest success?

He watched as his student, Nikolai Juma Das, inched sideways past the jutting rocks, hooked himself to the safety pole he had placed there last year and swung onto the terrace. It was a glaring cold day and the wind was blowing hard, spitting dirt in Nikolai's face and rolling treacherous cascades of pebbles beneath his feet. Canyons yawned all around him. But he made his report with calm formality, as though he were delivering a paper in an airtight classroom.

"On block 25-26, we planted pure South Dakota Abilene wheat alone," Nikolai said. "Nothing of that variety has survived from last year.

"On block 27-28, we planted Dante, a contemporary variety purchased from China; Motown, the most popular Crimean crop; and Galveston, a short season type that Professor Foster developed for the maritime provinces in eastern North America. Abilene, Dante, Motown and Galveston are all included among the many parent wheats of Waco. They have not germinated here. There is no sign of them anymore."

Nikolai slid along his ropes and stopped, hanging, to clean his wind goggles.

"We planted Waco in blocks 29 to 45," he said. He swung over to the edge of the next terrace, and slowly rounded the corner toward the 29-45 blocks, talking all the while. "Our hope is that, unlike its parents, Waco will have withstood the winter and broken the soil crust and started growing. And then we shall have what Professor Foster has been seeking since he came to Mongolia, a hardy bread wheat suited for the foothills of north central Asia."

Nikolai slipped past a huge boulder.

Stevie Foster closed his eyes.

"Look! Look!" the young man shouted, twirling in his ropes. "It's Waco!"

All through the frigid terraces, Stevie's students were cheering and jumping as they found lush stands of Waco wheat – short, robust, soon to be heavy with grain.

"Bravo, Professor!" Nikolai yelled.

For the Mongols who had accepted the loan of Stevie Foster from the Corporation for this project, it was a moment of delirious triumph. Pandemonium erupted in the viewing room. Officials of the University of the Wind hugged the blushing, breathless Texan and drank his health. The Minister of Agriculture got kind of carried away. "No more begging the Chinese for food loans!" he cried. "Screw the Empire! Chinguz lives!"

The news flashed outward to pertinent listeners and those who spied on them, all around the world.

It now appeared that the agreement to allow Chinese Beam readers into Mongolia would not be signed. A different agreement, permitting unprecedented Corporation access to Mongolian beamspace, would replace it.

Back in Minnesota, his grateful friends from the International Affairs Division presented Horatio Jedda with a rare bottle of scotch whiskey distilled from ancient unmodified barley grown during one season on a single field.

Horatio immediately shared it with Clyde Bright.

"This is your victory, Professor," he said, raising his glass.

The old professor sat beside Horatio on the front porch steps. One hundred and thirty-eight years old. Bleached white hair. Fierce blue eyes among the crinkles and wrinkles carved by sun and wind. Around his small farm house, a shining carpet of golden grain shimmied and billowed in the silky breeze and the sunshine. All 30 varieties authorized for cultivation in North America were growing here, each of them forever immune to rust.

Sure, the wheat belonged to the Corporation. But Horatio Jedda understood that in practice, in the working day-to-day, Dr. Clyde Bright was the big boss of every root and stalk.

There was no one in the world whom he admired more.

The old professor downed his whiskey and poured another and began to cry.

"My kid brother Eddie is out there someplace hiding from you bastards, and I'm sitting here with you, drinking the best booze on the planet."

"I'll bring him home," Horatio said. "I just need some time to overcome the opposition of certain people in the Meteorology Department."

"We grew up on a farm in Nebraska, did you know that? Of course you did. You know everything, don't you? Dad drove a gasoline-powered combine. He saved the seed from this year's crop to plant the next year. He grew what he wanted. He owned all of his land and his entire house. Gone. Gone. One brother. That's all I've got left."

"You have thousands of students," Horatio said. "You have The Grain Guardians. The love of a grateful continent."

"Not the same as a brother."

"I'll bring him home. I promise."

Clyde Bright set down his glass. He seemed suddenly to be listening to something. Some signal. He took a deep breath. He laid his white head on Horatio's shoulder.

"Ah. Too late," he said, and took another, longer, final breath.

Stevie Foster went to see Waco one last time before returning home to North America. The crop had just begun to head. Soon it would blanket the mountains in gold. Stevie had journeyed up to the hillside fields twice already, for he liked to experience Waco at every new stage of growth. Feeling sentimental, knowing how much he would miss his happy times at The University of the Wind, he canceled class and asked Nikolai Juma Das to sign out a suncopter for a third visit.

To man his high altitude project, Stevie had chosen students who came from the Alps and the Andes and the Rockies, who feared no height and breathed easily in thinner air. Nikolai -- the Himalayan kid -- was the best of them.

Twenty-two years old, lithe and powerful, a sunburned adventurer who climbed rocks like a salamander, he rode his horse to class and took the used lab rodents home to feed to his pet falcon. Next to one of his boots, he kept a long Chinese knife. Stevie had seen him butcher a rabbit with it and repair some pretty girl's sluggish Incoming with its gleaming tip. Once in the middle of a field lecture on soil chemistry, he had suddenly thrown it at a snake slithering toward the leg of a grazing horse. Nikolai's whistling knife had pinned the creature to the ground, saving the horse but also importantly saving the snake for dinner.

No one else in the class had noticed the danger.

Tenderly the Himalayan kid bent to collect samples of anything he found growing. A spray of oregano in the crack of a rock would stop him in his tracks. He fastened his straight black hair with some kind of bone. When he smiled, his black eyes narrowed to twinkling slits. He wore one earring and rimless goggles.

He told Stevie that at the age of fourteen, he had been forcibly recruited, along with other youngsters from the far corners of the Chinese Empire, to clear debris on the coast of the South China Sea, which had been devastated by a series of tsunamis.

While he was away, floods caused by melting glaciers drowned his family's fields back in Tibet.

Then the side of a mountain collapsed, becoming an avalanche of mud that drowned his family.

As he pulled the broken bodies of Chinese children from the rubble of Shanghai, Nikolai wept for his buried sisters.

When the rubble was cleared, the captured laborers were released with a bag of rice, a box of water and a tiny bit of money.

They went off in every direction, looking for friends, relations, any connection who might help them restart their interrupted lives. But Nikolai had no one.

He rode a crowded hoverbus as far north as it would take him. He could see the Wall twisting on the rims of the hills. Unlike the great dam, it still stood. *Millions of people, gone in days. And I mourned only for five lives in Tibet. Are all hearts so small, Professor?*

On a moonless night, he climbed up to the Wall, to the roadway where mighty armies had once passed with awful pomp. Silent as the dust, he slipped from crenellation to crenellation. Embedded sensors sometimes flooded him with light, making his heart jump and cringe. But nobody chased him. Nobody cared where he went.

On the other side of the Wall, he stole a hoverbike from a hut where a sick woman groaned. Rode twenty miles, then turned around, too disturbed by guilt to continue. When he got back to the house, the woman was dead. *So much for trying to make things right.*

He worked for food and a place to sleep, heading north. A farmer put him to work with the horses. They proved good company. The farmer's wife, a teacher, absorbed him into her school. It was embarrassing, to be sixteen and studying with kids two years younger, but Nikolai had long ago learned that humiliation didn't kill you. He stayed in the school for three years and graduated knowing two Mongol dialects, Mandarin, English, and horses.

The farmer died. His widow sold Nikolai to The University of the Wind. And the Agrotech Department there sold him to Stevie Foster.

"So you saved me, Professor," Nikolai said to Stevie in the crystal air between mountains.

"You saved yourself, kid," the Texan answered.

Unlike any other person Stevie knew, Nikolai possessed a mono-racial face. Most human beings had been so heterogenized by the 22nd century that racial typing had ceased to exist. In one family, siblings could range from eggshell to charcoal. A single individual could exhibit the traits of 100 cross global couplings. To see a face like Nikolai's – totally Tibetan – was a unique experience.

Of course, Stevie understood that Nikolai's astonishingly pure and ancient face was a function of the great Himalayan range. No matter how thoroughly these mountains had been invaded and colonized for thousands of years, they still hid valleys where living things could breed themselves in a separate ecosystem, the plants walled off from outside pollinators, the animals unthreatened by foreign predators, the women unloved by strangers.

"Who are you named for?" Stevie asked. "A Russian relative?"

"Oh no, all my relatives come from our valley. But many generations ago, back at the beginning of the 20th century, a Russian botanist passed through and made friends with one of my ancestors. I am named for him. Who are you named for, sir?"

"A song writer."

"And the wheat? For whom do you name your varieties of wheat?"

"For the lost cities of Texas."

"Was there a war in North America? When Texas seceded?"

"Dad thought there would be. He joined the Waco Rifles, ready for a big fight. He never dreamed that the Corporation would just let Texas go, like some beat-up sofa you set out by the road with a sign on it that says 'Free'. So no, Nikolai, there was no war. Nowadays dear old Texas is a free and independent wasteland. Galveston is drowned. Abilene is blown away. And Waco is growing in Mongolia."

Nikolai asked: "Do you ever go home?"

"No way. Too much sadness. All my people there are dead. Would you like to go home, kid? You could, you know. My contract guarantees my students six weeks of home leave every other year."

"I do not want to go. As you say, sir: too much sadness."

The suncopter flew them through mountain passes, past ancient shrines which had somehow survived the melt waters.

Excitedly, Stevie pointed out a family of four agile goats. A family, any family of anything, suggested that the old nature might be resurgent, a thrilling idea.

The wind was picking up. Black storm clouds boiled over the hills. The North American Beam had issued no storm warning, nor had Beijing or Ankara. Yet another sign of what Stevie considered the deteriorating state of meteorology. He wished Clyde Bright's brother were still broadcasting. "Eddie Bright, the Farmer's Friend." Now *he* had been a reliable weatherman. Stevie wondered what had become of him.

They landed on a south-facing slope, on the suncopter field constructed just for the Waco project. Nikolai helped his teacher with his ropes and offered his strong arm to hold as they launched themselves around the corner boulder.

Stevie Foster took one look at the wheat and his legs buckled. He exhaled a long groan.

"What is it, sir?"

Stevie didn't answer. He was sweating suddenly. His breathing sounded like weeping. Nikolai thought he might be having a heart attack.

"Please sir, what is it?"

Stevie staggered through the rows of grain. Brushed the heads with trembling hands. Peered closely at the stems. With his thumb nail, he scraped some powdery orange stuff off the stems.

"It's impossible," he murmured. "It doesn't exist anymore."

"What is it, sir?"

"Maybe I'm wrong. Maybe it's something else. I never saw it in the field, just pictures, just pictures...aw hell....the pictures looked just like this..." He crumpled to his knees like a loved one at a gravesite. Pulled his hat off his head, twisting it in his hands. "Get hold of Clyde Bright in Minnesota. He's the only one who still knows anything about rust."

3. THE JOURNEY NORTH

Uncle Furlong had rented a private hoverride to take me and Grandma on our vacation – a super treat seeing as folks on our continent never got to go anyplace alone.

Grandma was waiting for me at the restaurant, all six of her bags gathered around her like backup singers, and Shankar in his cage trilling like mad. The hover pulled itself right up in front of her. I leaped out and announced "Your ride is here, Madam!"

I loaded her stuff. She gave Paco El Din some last minute advice that I didn't hear, then wiggled into the passenger seat. And a big blonde tenor burst out from under a blanket in the back, singing *"Una furtiva lagrima."*

"Oh Cookie," Grandma sighed.

"How can I live for two weeks without you?" he actually cried. "What if you meet someone else and forget me?"

"Not to worry, darling. I forget nothing. Now would you please go and get me and my granddaughter a fizzy to drink on the road?" She looked up at him through her ginormous eyelashes and blinked. Irresistible. "Please?"

Cookie melted and ran off to get the fizzies. Grandma told the doors to lock and yelled "Go go go!"

We rose over the trees.

What a high, being driven by our own hover! I pressed all the buttons; flashed all the lights. The hover's Beam had been loaded with the cooking show, since Grandma as a restaurateur is considered a pertinent listener. Of course, we also received the Chairman's weekly message,.

We never hear the Chairman's own personal voice giving his message because his words are always expressed by some random shareholder. One week an old lady. The next week a boy with a lisp. It's the Chairman's way of showing that he speaks for all of us.

Personally I would rather have heard the Chairman himself, whoever he is, but that's just me.

On our journey north, we heard a gruff, military orderman type say: "This is your Chairman speaking. One. Due to the record-breaking harvest, rice allotments for shareholders between eight and twelve years of age will increase by one full ounce this week. Eat hearty, kids. Two. Those seeking seasonal algae gathering work should apply by Outgoing to Red Tide Info. Three. All the world's current wars are far away in Africa and the New Islands. We're at peace. We're eating regular. We're in profit. We're okay."

Right after the Chairman's message came the weather report, with Arliss.

Arliss started doing the weather just at the outset of the Era of Restored Order, when the Corporation was getting things under control and launching The Beam.

He was the one who replaced my Grandpa Eddie Bright as our main weatherman.

We all locked onto Arliss, without fail, because of course the weather report is pertinent to everybody. God, I had such a crush on him. He was one of the few men in North America who was actually taller than I was. I loved to watch his radiant smile and his big strong shoulders and his nice clean fingernails as he pointed to the moon and the stars. When Arliss made a mistake, everybody forgave him because he was so adorable.

As we were flying north, Grandma's Incoming kept flashing messages. A food critic was arriving in disguise tomorrow! The soprano didn't show! Someone broke in last night and stole Miss Piggy! All of these calls were blown off by Grandma. Finally the Incoming gave up. Shankar went to sleep. Wonderful silence. We were alone in our own hoverride. Amazing.

"So tell me how you met Grandpa," I said.

"How's about we just enjoy the silence."

"Come on, Grandma."

"I forget."

"You just told that crazy tenor, Mr. Cookie, that you forget nothing."

"Perhaps another time..."

"You promised."

"We lived in New York City," Grandma said. "A lovely island packed with tall buildings and good times. Oh Lizzie, if only you could have lived there then. Such good times.

"I came from a show biz family. Dad did lights. Mom painted costumes. Thank God they didn't live to see our city go under.

"For years and years, the weather had been getting hotter. There was a whole continent of ice at the top of the planet then, and it began to melt. So the oceans rose. The beaches around our city began to wash away. We had such beautiful beaches, Lizzie. We would go there in the summertime and eat hot dogs made of real pork and beef with mustard and..."

"Grandma."

"...saur kraut, that's real cabbage shredded and pickled and...God, there were French fries, Lizzie, these long skinny real potato pieces....and we dipped them in this divine red sauce call ketchup...oh God!"

"Grandma! Get a grip!"

"Yes yes okay okay sorry." She took a deep breath, patting her chest to calm herself. "Then these hurricanes began hitting us, one after the other. Waves as high as the landfill mountains. Wind like lions roaring. Rain that never stopped. We had to leave our city. Nine million people, all trying to get out.

"We used to drive private cars then. They ran on liquid fuel, not batteries, and they had wheels, which needed roads on the ground. But the roads washed out. The tunnels and the subways flooded. The airports closed down. The cars blew off the bridges like autumn leaves.

"The government sent boats. A lot of them sank. I crossed the river by hanging onto some wreckage. A nice boy helped me.

Good-hearted New Jersey folks took us in. Soon we ran out of food. If we found some, we would have to fight for it. We ate squirrels and dogs and waited for the food drop pilots to bring us powdered soy milk and peanut paste and tubes of water. I kept heading west, looking for a safe place.

"Then it stopped raining. No rain for months and months. It got to be burning hot. A flu that no one had ever seen before broke out. Oh my darling, that flu...people died from it in a couple of hours in front of your eyes, and you couldn't do anything. We were just helpless in the hands of nature.

"I hate nature.

"The government was running out of every kind of aid, and other countries couldn't help us because they were having it even worse. But then the Corporation came up with a vaccine and saved many of us. In other countries where there was no Corporation, millions and millions of people and animals just lay down and died.

"We were very grateful to the Corporation, darling. We were so grateful that we helped the Corporation win the revolution and become the government. And when they enacted the Fifteen Percent Deal, no taxes, no choices, just security, we said okay okay."

She paused. Frowned. Shook her head.

"When I think back to the time before the catastrophe," she said, "I realize we must have felt that it was coming. Because we had already begun to be much nicer to animals. We had stopped hunting them and eating them so much. It was like we had a feeling in our bones that everything alive would soon be in mortal danger, and so we wanted to make friends with other creatures."

I tried to understand this story she was telling me. Were they so helpless then? Couldn't they have done something?

"Maybe," Grandma said thoughtfully. "Maybe us kids could have prevented the destruction, if only we had risen up and demanded a change in the way the world was being used. But you know kids." She grinned and poked me. "They don't want to hear about hard times. They just tune out."

We rode in silence for a bit, Grandma lost in her reveries, me trying hard to imagine the world she had once known.

"How did you survive?" I asked. "When you were heading west..."

"I survived by singing."

"No kidding!"

"Once somebody gave me three chicken eggs just for a song to brighten the day. And I tried to stay looking good. It's easy for your mother to find that contemptible; after all, she has military training. And I was not some genius like Athena. I didn't have magic music ears like you that can hear birds chirping in the next town. I had a nice voice and mainly, to be honest, I was pretty. I did everything in my power to stay pretty, and I know that saved my life.

"I got a job in a club called 'The High Water Mark.' One night, thinking about all I had lost, I sat down at the piano there and sang a very bitter, angry song."

Grandma sang a verse of it.

> **We ran out of fuel,**
> **And we ran short of grain,**
> **The fish disappeared**
> **And so did the rain.**
> **Didn't you see that our shelves would be bare?**
> **Didn't you care?**

"I guess the song must have triggered some bad feelings," she said ruefully. "We had a crew of food drop pilots in the club that night, and they were drunk and ready to be disorderly, and they took the moonshine into the streets with them, singing my song. Soon there was a mob. And such a rage, Lizzie, such a terrible rage. Because I had lost two...just too much...and we knew, all this calamity was no accident. *It had been done to us.* By the generations of plenty. They just kept ignoring the signs and using and wasting and destroying everything in the world so there was nothing left for us, and if we found an old person, we blamed them, we beat them up, we were like the wrath of God." She took a long ragged breath. "Some of them died.

"The ordermen came. There was a big fight. We all ended up in jail. "Grandpa was in my cell. He told me I was the herald angel who sings the anthem that brings the new world. I would have flown off with him as soon as we were released. But a man from the Corporation, with a lovely smile and a big moustache, he took me out and fed me a wonderful dinner and offered me a job singing jingles.

"It was good money, darling, and finally, safe harbor. All I had to do was give up 85% of myself and promise never to sing another dangerous song.

"I became a success and married Grandpa Arnie and had your Uncle Furlong. The Corporation began providing us with synthetic food that they had invented in their labs. The earth quieted down a little. Things got better.

"I didn't see Eddie Bright again until I was a widow, and we were both working on the old public web. He walked into the studio and said 'Hi there, angel. Remember me?'"

We glided past the picturesque ruins of San Francisco, then northward over the New Dead Sea.

Uncle Furlong had told us that the New Dead Sea started out in the 20th century as a runoff pond where the chemicals that farmers used to put on their crops could be dumped as the rain washed them out of the fields. Eventually the water in the pond evaporated. The remaining chemicals crystallized into star-shaped towers.

The supersmart techs in the Chemical Division figured out how to make the crystal towers into waterproof glue that could help to reassemble broken machines. But then one night, the glue exploded in its storage tanks, poisoning the air and forcing the evacuation of several seaside towns. Since no one could live in them anymore, the Corporation built a wall around the towns, then dug a canal to let the ocean come in and cover them, then closed off the canal, creating a poisoned lake which is now known as the New Dead Sea.

From where Grandma and I hovered above, we could get a good look at the brined houses through the clear water. The water certainly didn't look dangerous. It looked perfectly fine.

Suddenly I heard flapping.

"Something's coming, Grandma. Listen."

"I don't hear anything."

The flapping was getting closer. And something was screaming.

"It's coming from the east, Grandma. Flapping and screaming."

"I don't hear a thing, darling. Perhaps you're im…"

"Hold on!"

I grabbed her and held her tight as the hover shook and plunged in a rush of turbulence. A ginormous bird passed the window, huge wings flapping the air around us and the sea below us into terrifying waves. He had a bald head and silver neck feathers and a screaming rat in his beak.

He dropped the rat into the New Dead Sea. I looked down. The creature was trapped on the surface, unable to sink, writhing in agony, dissolving inch-by-inch in the killer waters.

The bird vanished over the horizon. Grandma and I clung to each other, shaking. Our hover steadied itself and headed for Oregon and The Ashland Wet Spot.

4. THE ASHLAND WET SPOT

Our room at The Ashland Wet Spot had a window that faced an actual forest. It was so beautiful, I could not stop gazing at it. Shankar alighted on my hand, and he couldn't stop gazing at it either.

I counted at least ten different kinds of trees: not just green ones but grayish and reddish and bluesy, with needles, with berries, round leaves, pointy leaves, with pods dangling. Some of those trees were twice as tall as me!

As evening approached, they shimmered and waved like ghost dancers, lit by the moon.

Grandma insisted that we dress for dinner.

She had 27 outfits to choose from. I had my long black or my short blue.

"Not to worry, darling," she said. "Before this vacation ends, you're going to be the best dressed girl in the northwest."

Eight other people shared our table. Most were older than Grandma. They objected to Shankar sitting on her shoulder until they realized that he was a supersmart bird, personally fastidious, who sweetly ate cracker crumbs from your palm and only pooped in designated trash receptacles. The waiter, thrilled to spot someone his own age, flirted with me until I stood up.

Many of the old folks remembered Grandma from the days of the public web, and they begged her to sing their favorites. Sweet songs. Sentimental songs. None of those tough songs of the war years – *Let us right the grievous wrongs, And rescue what belongs, To us!* - or the sad songs of the famine times – *Close your eyes, my child, and go, To heaven where the clean streams flow...* God. Soooooh depressing.

Grandma sang "In the Gloaming" and other calm, soft songs to suit The Era of Restored Order in which we are lucky enough to live right now.

One of the gladiators, a heavyweight wrestling champion named Sunshine Gomez, lumbered up to the stage with a girl-shaped clay drum. He said he had inherited it from his Armenian grandfather, and it always brought him luck. The drum had a flat, Middle Eastern tone that sounded a little bit aggressive next to Grandma's schmaltzy, Irish-type numbers. But still, a drum. Kept the beat. Imitated the heart. Made Shankar dance.

Clearly Sunshine was falling in love with Grandma. I told him Grandma was more than three times his age. He didn't care. He just kept bringing her glasses of wine and telling her how beautiful she was. (God, it's annoying when Aunt Petunia's predictions come true.)

As she got drunker, Grandma began singing songs I had never heard her sing before. They got people very excited. When she started belting out "Salted Dog", and some ladies with a background in the theatre climbed up on tables and began taking off their clothing, the hotel orderman showed up to close down the show.

"One more," pleaded Grandma. "Just one more song." She looked up at the orderman through her lashes. "Please?"

He melted, exactly like Cookie the tenor. The crowd quieted.

"My granddaughter Elizabeth will sing this one," Grandma said. "Ladies and gentlemen, Lizzie Corelli."

I sang "Believe Me, If All Those Endearing Young Charms."

Not a dry eye in the house.

I guess the people were thinking about the lyrics and about not being forgotten or less-loved, even now that they were old and maybe singing their final songs.

The manager of the hotel asked me if I would sing every night in exchange for the elimination of our room fee. (*My first professional job outside of the agroclan world! Yayyy!*) I tried to remain calm, not daring to look at Grandma, who was glowing with pride so brightly she could have powered the kitchen. I said I would perform on condition that the manager hire my accompanist. He agreed and immediately set about making arrangements for Paco El Din to join us at the Ashland Wet Spot.

As soon as Grandma and I were alone, I said "I've got to get something pretty to wear!"

Shankar flew around the hotel, befriending everybody, gobbling up irritating bugs. We never let him fly outside because he might get lost in the forest and die there. Whenever we went on an adventure, we locked him into his cage.

Grandma signed us up for massages and gym classes, the soothing chembaths and a white water canoe trip on the Peaceful Conduct River. The prospect of that terrified me. "Not to worry, darling," Grandma said. "When I was a girl, we did it for sport, and it was free."

At the Ashland Wet Spot, it was really expensive.

Our captain, Oglethorpe, seated himself in the center of a big double hulled canoe and took up his oars. He was a short guy, heavier set than anybody I had ever seen, a physique mandated, he declared, by the Samoan genes on his father's side. Half-naked, greased up and tattooed all over, Oglethorpe wore necklaces of shells and bracelets of clicketing clacketing seeds around his wrists and ankles. His long oiled hair was braided and coiled into a top knot.

"This is how they did it back in King Kamehameha's times," Oglethorpe told us. "They rode over the ocean in canoes that were lashed together in pairs, with only the wind in their sails and their oars for power, looking for more of the earth, because they had not seen it all then, and they thought it was endless."

The idea that anybody would think this teensy planet was endless just made me laugh.

The other passengers besides me and Grandma included two gladiators with huge muscles and smashed up ears. One seemed exhausted, the other up-tight and watchful. Also we had Sally, a frowsy blousy woman with waggledy arm flesh. She said she was

117 years old. Lots of wrinkles. Big pores. Wild scraggledy eyebrows, white and blonde and gray like her flyaway hair. Almost no lips, which gave her a tight tense angry look, like she had endured many hardships.

She wouldn't shake Grandma's hand.

"I remember you," she said. "You were the one who started the riot."

Grandma looked puzzled and utterly innocent. "Excuse me?"

"Singing that song. At 'The High Water Mark'."

"I don't remember."

"Let's not be coy here, missus. I remember and so do you. I had just signed on with the ordermen. Mostly because I didn't have anything to wear and they would give me a uniform. You started that riot, and instead of going to jail, you somehow went straight to the old public web. Blood in the streets, and there you were, in sequins."

Grandma sighed. "It was ninety-five years ago, Sally."

"How many old people died in that riot? Two hundred? Two fifty?"

I gasped. Grandma hadn't exactly described the true death toll when she said "Some of them died."

Captain Oglethorpe ended this awful exchange by suddenly stowing his oars and announcing "Safety time."

He hung a little blue ball around each passenger's neck.

"Each ball contains a boat that will self-inflate and float you to safety in case you are swept overboard," he said. "It's a ridiculous precaution because in ten years leading canoeing trips at this hotel, not one of my passengers has ever landed in the water."

I had never seen a real rushing river before. Of course, little streams, made by a rain shower before the water was trapped for drinking -- but not a mighty river, cascading over rocks, making waterfalls and whirlypools. Amazing.

I settled in the back of the canoe where I could stretch out and dangle my feet in the water. Captain Oglethorpe objected. "I like all my passengers seated up front where I can see them."

"But I'm too squishy up there."

"But you are too spread out back there. Don't like my passengers dangling."

For the first time in my life I did what Grandma does when she wants something from some guy. I smiled and looked up at Captain Oglethorpe through my lashes and said, "Please?" He was supposed to melt and give in, like the hotel orderman and Cookie the tenor. Instead, he commanded me to climb to the front of the canoe or be forcibly transported back to the hotel.

"Maritime law requires absolute obedience to the captain, young lady, and I am the captain of this vessel."

I had no choice but to squeeze myself between the bulging muscles of the gladiators.

Oglethorpe rowed. The canoe glided. Soon the hotel docks had disappeared, and all we could hear was water slurping on the oars, bugs humming and real birds chirping.

I counted fifteen different bird songs, in all different keys and in rhythms I had never even imagined before. Wouldn't it be amazing if there were a way to get the birds to chime in during my act…like for harmony…or as a percussion section… And the frogs! Maybe I could use the croaking frogs as back-up altos.

Sunlight flashed on the leaves of bushes on the shore. Grasses waved from the banks. Little white beaches gleamed. Actual fish splashed.

I began to sing one of Grandma's old songs about a river. *Where are you going, my sweetsie fair?* The exhausted gladiator put his head on Grandma's lap and slept, smiling… *just down by the river, down by the spring…* dreaming of his true love, I suppose. The other gladiator didn't move except for his eyes, watching one shore, then the other. *See the wild rippling water, hear the nightingale sing….*

Sally sat hunched over, scowling.

"You know," she said, "in the end of that song, he dies."

48

Then the rapids hit us.

A sudden jolt. Violent bouncing. Ice cold spray smacked us. The sleeping gladiator woke up and cried "Gloria!"

Grandma screamed. "My hair is getting wet!"

"What the hell, Oglethorpe," Sally yelled. "Get control of this tub!"

Oglethorpe said: "No problem, Major. In ten years leading canoeing trips at this hotel, not one of my..." and we plunged over a waterfall and went flying.

I tumbled and choked in the bubbling water. It flipped me, smashed me against rocks, tore off my shoes, bounced me from one submerged tree trunk to another, and whenever I tried to right myself, it turned me upside down, pinned my limbs to my body or spun them in crazy loopdies. Slimy stems wrapped around my neck. I flipped and folded and unfolded and popped to the surface. My safety opened into a clear-eyed little boat and floated me, dazed, legs dangling.

We had somehow entered a placid section of the river. I looked up at the fluffy clouds rolling by. Grandma had abandoned her safety boat. She was swimming toward me. (I had no idea that Grandma was such a strong swimmer. I guess that's how she escaped from New York.) "Not to worry, Lizzie darling," she hollered. "I'm on my way!"

Her face came lunging up over the side of my little boat. She felt my head, gasped at the bruises and scratches on my legs and arms, then turned and, hauling me behind her, she side-stroked in the direction of one of the small white beaches.

On the far side of the water, I could see Sally paddling herself to another beach with the two gladiators close behind. But where was Oglethorpe and the canoe?

We sat on the sand, catching our breath.

Grandma extracted a style'n'spray tube from her underwear and began putting her bob back together. Even for her, that seemed a bit much. I mean really, in the middle of the wilderness, after you've nearly been drowned...come on...

But then an old man stepped out of the forest, and Grandma fell into his arms. So I guess she must have known what she was doing.

He bent her over backwards and kissed her pretty much endlessly. It would have been a sexy moment except that I could hear Grandma's vertebrae scrunching.

She emerged breathless and said "Lizzie darling, this is your grandfather, Eddie Bright. Eddie, this is our Lizzie."

He was an unhappy looking man, sunburned and rumpled, with messy white hair and thick glasses. He wore his gray work shirt buttoned to his chin and white socks with his sandals.

He looked up at me.

"Your grandmother told me you were big," he said. "But I didn't expect gigantic."

Grandma groaned. "Oh Eddie!"

"And I didn't expect to dislike you right away," I said. "But somehow I do."

He hugged me. I was glad that he hugged me, but truth be told, he was so strong that his hug hurt.

That, in essence, is the thing with Grandpa.

He sighed and sat down on a rock. He said: "My big brother Clyde dropped dead last week."

Grandma cried out: "Oh honey, that's terrible, I'm so sorry..." Then wistfully: "God, it's lucky to just drop dead." (Old people say the most peculiar things sometimes.)

"I didn't know," Grandpa Eddie continued. "I called from a safe Outgoing just to say Hi. A Corporate message comes on, with this woman, she says she's Mrs. Esmerelda Wolf, she's in charge of Clyde's stuff, a face like granite and gray braids wrapped around her head. She says she's sorry to report that Professor Bright has passed away.

"If I hadn't called, I wouldn't have known. The man was dead a week before they even put a message on his Outgoing. A great professor, hundreds of discoveries, thousands of students, and he dies and...silence. Do you know want to know why? Because 85% of everything Clyde accomplished is owned by the Corporation, and they needed a week to go through his house and his labs and make sure he hadn't hidden anything from them. Only after they were done with all that, only then can those of us who cared about the man gather together and drink to his memory and throw him a funeral!"

Grandpa's weathered face had turned dark. Each white whisker stood out like a thorn. Grandma wrapped her arms around him and leaned against his back, whispering "Shhh, my darling...shhh... He was a great man. We'll have a memorial service. It'll be packed. Lizzie and I will go. Evangeline will fly in from NewLA. Lizzie will sing. Wait'll you hear our Lizzie sing."

"How can I miss my own brother's funeral, Foxie?" he asked miserably. "How can I not carry his coffin?"

Then out of the blue, Shankar showed up. He hopped onto my finger, tweeting and trilling.

"Hey, how did you get out of your cage, smarty beaks? I know we locked it. And how'd you find us in this big wilderness?" I tickled his rosy belly. He ruffled his scarlet feathers and fluttered over to Grandma's hair. I guess it must have been sticky from the style'n'spray. I guess his teensy bird feet must have gotten stuck. Because Grandpa had time to grab him and tear off his head.

Grandma and I screamed.

Printed circuits, already self-destructing, spilled out of the little red body along with absolutely no blood.

"Go go go run!" Grandpa yelled.

He tossed both pieces of Shankar into the Peaceful Conduct River, and they exploded.

"Who gave you that bird?!" Grandpa yelled.

"The the the cook," Grandma managed.

"For her birthday!" I added.

"How could you accept a pet as a gift?! Don't you realize Horatio Jedda uses robot animals as spies? They're connected to his agents, circuit for neuron. Your little red bird was programmed to lead the Corporation right to me."

We were speechless. It is true that when a person is right, they are right and you have to give them credit for that. But you also have to recover from them being right, and that took a couple of minutes. I couldn't help myself, I started to cry. "We loved that bird!"

"Well then you are clearly as much of an idiot as your grandmother," snapped Eddie Bright.

"Oh Eddie," Grandma lamented. "Just because you think the Corporation is trying to kill you doesn't mean you get to behave like an asshole."

I stomped off through the forest onto the shore road, and there was Paco El Din, sitting on a tree stump, plunking "Midnight's Special" on the banjo.

"They flew me in this morning," Paco said. "You look kind of down."

"I just met my grandfather. He turns out to be mean and ill-tempered. Shankar turned out to be some kind of a spy or something. It's all too much."

"Where's Mrs. Burton Bright?"

"Back on the beach with Grandpa. Looks like they really love each other. Too bad they couldn't stay married. Too bad he can't just move back in with her. He says he can't even go to Great Uncle Clyde's funeral."

"It's not real safe. He's got to hide."

"Would they arrest him?"

"They would most likely just make him disappear. You can't never know with the Corporation. We had a farmhand who was working off his parole in the corn fields. He liked to grab a lamb every year to treat his family on the holidays. I was working long side him on the hoverreaper, and I heard this whining sound, and the next thing I knew a drone bullet from nowhere had killed him. The bullet was engraved with a charge message. It said STEALING FROM THE CORPORATION."

"But weren't they your father's sheep?"

"They were. And my daddy would never have hurt that man. But everything we think we own is really owned by the Corporation. We just get to buy a share. That's the system, Miss Lizzie. Your Uncle Furlong. My daddy. They may look rich, but they're still just part owners. When you and I get bought by the Bloomington Music School, we'll be part owners of ourselves."

"But why is the Corporation so angry at Grandpa? He didn't steal anything."

"Yes, he did. He stole the attention of the people, for purposes of telling the truth."

I finally realized I was not talking to an ordinary farm boy with a musical gift.

"Is this a group thing, Paco? I mean, are you *with* Grandpa?"

"Yes ma'am. I am. So are lots of other folks. Are you?"

Sally arrived, wet and mad as hell, riding in an official blue orderman hoverride. The watchful gladiator was driving.

"Something exploded."

"Oh, is that what that sound was? Is everybody okay? This is my accompanist, Paco. He just got here."

"Where's your grandfather?"

"You mean my grandmother. She's taking a dump in the woods." (To this day, I cannot believe I actually said that about my own dear Grandma.)

"We were just practicing our act, ma'am," Paco said. "Care to hear?"

He looked into my eyes.

"Let's do an 'Aunt Rhodey Round the Mountain' combo," I said. "E-minor. Loud and lusty. You sing too."

He turned his volume up as high as it could go.

Everybody anywhere near the river shore had to have heard us shouting out those crazy old songs.

I admit, I tweaked the lyrics just a bit.

Go tell Aunt Rhodey,
The old gray goose is here.
She'll be comin' round the mountain,
She'll be ridin' by the river...

Sally closed her meaty hand over Paco's strings. "That's enough of that, mister. Where's Oglethorpe?"

I gasped with horror. "Is he missing? Our captain? Was he hurt in the explosion? God. Is it possible he drowned?" Thinking *I'll bet you anything Captain Oglethorpe did not drown.*

Grandma walked out of the woods with a little harvest gathered in her skirt. "Look what I found. Real blackberries, just growing all by themselves. Good to see you, Paco darling. Oh. Hi Sally. I hope it wasn't illegal to pick them. They are *so* delicious! Who wants some? How's about we take a few back to the hotel for our little bird Shankar."

5. GRAIN GUARDIANS

IN THE LAB

Normally, the Grain Guardians were separated by great distances and communicated only on closely-watched and censored screens. Clyde Bright's funeral, however, brought them together in the flesh. Thus, it happened that they were all gathered in one lab when Stevie Foster and his assistant, Nikolai, delivered the rust-infected wheat from Mongolia.

Stevie had aged and wilted under the weight of Waco's failure. All strength seemed to have left his body. His colleagues were shocked by the look of him and by his terrible news.

"Did the rust spread to every plant?" Itamar Mugombo asked.

"Every single one."

"Did the Mongols allow any to mature?"

"No. They made a genomic analysis, buried it in code, and destroyed the crop. Far as I know, what you see before you is the only remnant."

Itamar patted his old friend's shoulder. He was a tall, skinny, dark brown man, with a wedge of stiff silver hair and the limb articulation of a praying mantis. Ordinarily, he worked in the burning sands of the Mohave Spread, so re-named because the Mohave Desert had spread by miles in every direction during the previous 100 years and showed no signs of stopping. Unused to the brisk chill of Minnesota, he had wrapped himself in several shawls.

"Were there storms?" he asked. "High winds?"

"Yeah there were. They caught us by surprise 'cause of the bad weather reporting. Take away the satellites, and meteorology reverts to rumor and guesses."

"So maybe it maybe it maybe ummmm...maybe the rust blew in from somesomesome someplace else." Felicity Bjornsdottir spoke in a childishly high-pitched voice.

"But we had no word of infections," Stevie said. "Not from Russia, China, Turkey. This rust must not have been hungering for their varieties. It was hanging up there in the clouds." He sighed miserably. "Waiting for my Waco."

Felicity chewed the end of her long yellow braid and cast her pale blue gaze upward, a sign of serious thought. "Did you happen to see any ummm any ummm any ummm uh..."

Her friends tried to help her.

"Migrating snow geese."

"Long-haired goats."

"No no b...b..."

Stevie put his arm around her. His arm would only go so far. Felicity Bjornsdottir was extremely fat. "You gotta try and relax, honey," he said.

"B...b...b...barberry bushes!" Felicity finally shouted. "Did you see any wild barberry bushes in the area?"

"Maybe I wasn't looking," Stevie admitted.

She turned to the Himalayan kid. "Nikolai?"

"Professor Bjornsdottir, forgive me, I am a stranger to all this, I have never heard of this barberry."

"Stem rust is a fungus," Itamar explained. "It spreads by spores, on the wind, in a downpour, on a down draft, in the fur and feathers of animals and birds, even on the clothing of farmers. The spores usually reproduce on their own. But sometimes they blow into a wild barberry bush and reproduce sexually with a spore from a different race of rust. Then quite suddenly, one is presented with a new race. Your variety of wheat may be immune to the old race, but it will be helpless against the new one."

"And there goes the harvest," Stevie said.

"Clyde Bright's rust immunity genes have protected all 340 wheat varieties authorized for growing in the world today. No one has seen the fungus for 70 years. We thought it was extinct, like tomatoes and zebras."

"They did something to my brains in that place," Felicity mumbled. "Now I forget I just forforfor..."

Under cover of a security blackout, the Grain Guardians set about infecting the authorized 340 with the stem rust that had attacked Waco, hoping to find some that would prove immune. First the 30 for North America, then the 18 for Anatolia, 21 for Central Europe and on and on.

Their researches were quickened by the great advances in visualization which had transformed science during the previous century and a half. Lab equipment to enter and observe cells in action had become standard. The Grain Guardians could literally stand inside each wheat variety as it was being attacked. They could see the disease being born long before it would achieve virulence and appear on the plant's stem.

Microbial particles of rust knocked on the walls of the wheat cells. Pushing. Pushing. Beating against the pliant cells of the healthy grain.

In five minutes, Clyde Bright's resistance genes began fighting back, trying to disable the invader.

In ten minutes, the resistance genes were overcome, and the red demon was spreading unobstructed through the life systems of the wheat.

All 340 fell before the onslaught. No survivors.

Stevie had considered naming the new stem rust "M" for May in Mongolia. However, Itamar, watching the fungus at work, was reminded of the venomous female spiders that lurked around his desert greenhouses, how they mated with their male partners and then devoured them. So he feminized "M" and called her EMMY. The St. Paul lab would in future become known as "EMMYHQ", as though it were a restaurant. One customer. Lots of meals.

Stevie's Incoming buzzed.

"Is there something we should know about, Dr. Foster?" said Esmerelda Wolf. (As Eddie Bright had noted to Foxie and Lizzie, she did indeed have a face like granite, and stern gray braids chained her head.)

"Maybe not just quite yet, Mrs. Wolf," said Stevie. "We've gotta organize some thoughts here. Please could you tell Horatio we'll call when we're sure of our results."

Jedda did not wait. Fifteen minutes later, he showed up in person. He entered the lab so quietly that the Grain Guardians didn't even know he was there until he coughed. "

"Ah Horatio, forgive us for not calling. We have a bit of a problem."

"Talk plain, Itamar," said Stevie. "This is real serious, Horatio. We found a new variety of wheat stem rust. Kills everything."

"Define everything."

"All the wheat now grown in the world."

Jedda uttered a sigh. Not exactly a sigh. More like an ironic little snuffle. "So that's what they were looking for... After your great success with Waco, Professor Foster, your research was stolen by our competitors in Beijing, as usual. Four Chinese agrobots disguised as mountain goats visited your fields in Mongolia, presumably to collect samples. Three missed their footing and tumbled into the chasms, which was how we knew they weren't real mountain goats. The fourth several transmissions before we captured him. We are still trying to decode those transmissions. I assume they concern this current problem."

"But this is great!" Stevie exclaimed. "If the Chinese have EMMY, then our chances for finding a control are way better! We've gotta alert the scientific community! Work together with Chow Sam and his lab! Pool our data!"

"You should get some rest, Professor," Jedda said. "Your eyes are red with exhaustion. And look, your assistant is out cold."

True enough. Nikolai lay collapsed under a lab table, snoring.

"P..p...please, Horatio, think please," Felicity pleaded. "Maybe um maybe uh maymaymay um..."

"Honey," Stevie said.

"Maybe fifty people on earth know anything about stem rust," she continued. "We need themallthemallthem…"

"If the fungus flies east to China, that is a third of the world's wheat in mortal danger right there," Itamar said. "Our data could help them defend their crop."

"Think. P..p…p…please."

"If it flies west, it could infect the Kazakh harvest. From there it could reach Ukraine and then Russia."

"The wheat crop of Russia!" Felicity pleaded, quoting one of her favorite ancient seers. "'*One of the great economic facts, which underlie all the activities of men, in peace or war.*'"

"Surely you can see…"

"We've gotta share everything we know…"

"We m-m-must collabcollabcollab… "

"I'll get right on it," Horatio Jedda said.

IN THE NIGHT

Horatio went home to his standard 600-square foot apartment and drank some of the whiskey he had shared with Clyde Bright. His black spaniel puppy, Pepper, sat at his feet. *We can't let the famine happen again. If it does, we will kill each other so much that we will make ourselves as extinct as honey bees. We have to have a plan.*

All night, he listened to Brahms, thinking.

At the start of the 21st century, the planet had been staggering from the pressure of human over-population. Experts agreed that ten billion people would swarm the earth by 2075. Instead, a global correction, triggered by climate change, had reduced the human population to a scant four billion, with barely enough resources left to sustain them. All political power in the world was now based on the control and distribution of food.

Where the government was the enemy of the people, starvation persisted, and conflicts erupted like geysers. The North American Corporation system, of which Horatio was a dedicated exponent, had done a better job than most keeping the people fed and the apparatus that controlled them unobtrusive.

Science, which expected always to go forward, had been slowed to a near halt by the catastrophes. Precious libraries of books and music, seeds and tissue samples and formulae, museums for art, for film and video, networks of circuits and servers that could access vast clouds of data, all fell victim to angry nature, which avenged itself on people by wiping away their history.

The great seed saver Felicity Bjornsdottir warned her students that the destruction had made scholars susceptible to "re-failure", that they might easily ignore the great instructive breakthroughs and setbacks of the past. Look how completely the work of Brother Gregor Mendel, the father of genetics, had been forgotten until -- by a stroke of good fortune – it was rediscovered years after his death. Could the remnant of humanity afford such painful mistakes now in these hard times? No, said Felicity. And her boss, Horatio Jedda, agreed.

The only answer was to save everything. Every little scrap of surviving agricultural wisdom must be saved.

History, that wrecked and blasted dust bin, would as ever emerge as the source of the future.

The antidote to EMMY would be found, Horatio concluded, in some ancient snip of the buried past.

For starters, he ordered an immediate hold-and-review on all the Grain Guardians' communications, Incoming and Outgoing. Didn't want them alarming the whole world just yet.

The Turks were beset by the surprise reappearance of crop-choking wild mustard, long believed eradicated. The Indians were fighting an invasion by millions of cat-sized vegetarian rats. The Russian bread basket could look forward to a fine harvest as long as the chlorophyll-sucking aphid stayed killed. Why upset all these busy farmers with news of a distant threat from a flying fungus, which might or might not turn into big trouble?

Fortunately, no North American wheat field lay in EMMY's immediate path, a geographical accident that allowed more time to search for a defense strategy.

Wheat was one of the few crops that had survived from the old nature with something like its original purposes intact. Now that mining and drilling had been outlawed everywhere to minimize the danger of earthquakes, and most forests were brand new, basic materials had to be reinvented through the miracles of bioengineering. Rice made walls, floors and furniture. Cassava made masonry. Corn wove clothing, bedding and anything else requiring fiber, replacing wool, as rare as sheep now, and cotton and flax (and of course silk), which had completely disappeared. Everything once formed in plastic now came from potatoes. Tobacco piggybacked drugs and cleaning products. Genetically commingled with precious samples of real plants from the old nature, soy had become the preferred building block for the synthetic foods that now fed everybody.

Manure, whose precious gas might once have powered the earth, was now as rare as milk cows, not to speak of cattle on the hoof. It had to be hoarded, since supplies of other natural fertilizers had been exhausted, and the unnatural ones had been outlawed.

However, wheat, though changed by science, still made bread, pasta, cereal, feed for animals. Clever farmers scrambled to replace the yield that had been destroyed by war and weather. They grew it in every tiny yard, on rooftops, *as* rooftops, on the old highway beds under the hoverroads, on fields set one above the other in staggered stacks like pancakes, rotating to catch the sun and share the rain.

Stevie Foster had even taught them to grow it on mountains.

A deadly plague on the wheat crop could return the continent to famine, and blast away the delicate balance of cost and price, requirement and reward that placated the population and prevented another revolution.

Where had the rust come from?

Why had fate resurrected it to bedevil humanity once again?

Why the hell did Clyde Bright have to drop dead just when the Corporation needed him most?

Horatio slept in his chair.

Pepper woke him at dawn, as programmed, licking his face. He patted the dog and smiled insofar he was able to smile.

He had a plan.

He figured there were two ways to beat EMMY.

The short way was chemical.

Horatio would task the Chemical Division with developing an EMMY-specific fungicide pellet to kill the plague. Although applied agrocides of every sort had long ago been banned and the leftovers destroyed in favor of genetic disease control, it was still possible to imbue an aero-pellet with a good old-fashioned poison. Pop the pellet into the field, activate the solar battery, and EMMY-killer would radiate for miles around, stopping the fungus dead the moment she threatened the wheat plants.

He calculated that with some additional staff, the chemtechs would have his fungicide pellets up and running in a couple of weeks. By the time EMMY spread, the Corporation would be ready to sell them to desperate farmers everywhere.

The long way was genetic.

He would send Felicity Bjornsdottir back to Antarctica with instructions to find genes for resistance to EMMY among the untold thousands of varieties of wheat, new, ancient, wild, as well as untold thousands more wheat relatives like rye and triticale and goat grass, that were stored in the germplasm bank.

As a back-up, he would instruct Itamar to search the desert sands for microscopic remnants of ancient wheat which might contain EMMY resistance.

Once the resistance genes were found, Stevie Foster would breed them into each North American type, and when he was done with that, he would do the same for the varieties used by the rest of the world. That was how Norman Borlaug had done it in the 1960s in Mexico; that was how Clyde Bright had done it in the 2060s in Minnesota; that was how the Grain Guardians would do it today.

As soon as the 340 authorized varieties of resistant seed were in hand, the Corporation would sell them, over and over again every year, to desperate farmers everywhere.

Another "Jedda Bonanza." This one could get him elected as the next Chairman.

Tending his tiny greenhouse, misting his broccolish and his carroteens, Horatio considered how much simpler these decisions would be if he could know which way the wind would blow EMMY.

He had no faith in the Meteorology Department and their mascot, that grinning matinee idol, Arliss. A mere actor, a lightweight. The Chairman found him amusing. But this emergency demanded a *real* weatherman, with historical models and seasoned instincts and a dedication to accuracy, someone with friends in literally high places, like mountain tops all over the world, who would watch and report and share observations. If only he could keep his promise to Clyde Bright and lure his brother Eddie off the radical fringe.

Horatio had assigned a good cook with a red bird to infiltrate Eddie Bright's ex-family. Too bad the wily old weatherman had spotted the bird as a spy and killed it. Before his death, however little Shankar had amassed some useful information.

Horatio now knew how much Eddie still loved Foxie Burton Bright.

He knew about Evangeline.

And Lizzie.

AT THE MUSEUM

Revived by half a night's sleep on the floor of the lab, rewarded with a break from the deliberations of the bigwigs, Nikolai pocketed his per diem and set out on foot to explore the capitol of North America, St. Paul, Minnesota.

The city did not at first seem strange to him. In fact St. Paul reminded him of Beijing. Low blocks of 600 square foot apartments, judged to be adequate living space in a society with so few children. Construction materials printed on cellulosic board, heavy enough to shelter, light enough to collapse harmlessly when the next earthquake hit. Compact wind turbines on the rooftops; tiny greenhouses instead of windows; multi-colored people riding hoverbuses, nibbling all manner of high nutrition pick-me-ups which had replaced regular meals everywhere. On random walls and underfoot, embedded cameras and recorders lurked, a stealthy presence one dared not forget.

However, the lilacs surprised him. He had never seen so many, such a vast array of colors. The North Americans must be a sensual, spendthrift race, he thought, to waste so much fertile soil on a plant that produced no food, no shelter, no fuel but only pretty flowers and an intoxicating smell.

And the dogs! They were everywhere. Apparently people here preferred not to eat them but rather to keep them as companions.

Nikolai had once loved a dog, a mastiff mutt named Oberon. *Why did I give him that name? Oh yes, because we were studying Shakespeare in school when he was born. Oberon, King of the Fairies.* A dangerous, loving dog, Oberon sank his teeth into the leg of the soldier who was hauling away his friend. *Let him go, boy. Get away, go home, they'll kill you.* Beaten off with clubs, bleeding, Oberon never whimpered. He just kept barking.

It was better not to think of Oberon.

Nikolai bought a fizzy drink that made him burp and a fruit called an appleish and headed for the AgMuseum, a red stone mound of a building, constructed to resemble an ancient soddy, that rose from the ground on the site of the old plant pathology department at the University. The lady at the desk told Nikolai that nobody visited much anymore. Maybe some agrotech students who had just been bought at auction, assigned to write a history paper. Maybe some veterans in their 150s, last survivors of The Generation of Plenty, dragging their great-great-grandchildren for a look at the vanished old nature.

"You'll find the exhibits personally interactive and quite exhilarating," the lady said. "Here's your guide to the buttons. We don't allow eating materials in the museum. You can leave your snacks here with me. That will be 75 cents North American."

The Museum's central chamber had a single ocular window at the center of its rounded roof and a few chairs gathered in the long ray of light it sent to the floor below. Nikolai sat in one of the chairs, selected "Wheat Rust" from the directory, pressed a button and entered history.

He walked through the ruined wheat fields of ancient Rome and attended the sacrifice of red animals — foxes and certain heifers -- to appease the rust god. He hid from rampaging East African mobs, whose wheat fields had been destroyed by rust, as they hacked their neighbors to death with machetes to get at their stored grain. On a Mexican street, he stood shoulder to shoulder with a gang of proud scientists who had once helped to defeat the rust for a while.

He pressed one button after another.

Russia. 1897. In the fields, men chopped wheat with scythes. Women and children bent over double to gather it into bundles. Among them Nikolai met an American with a broad-brimmed hat and a long moustache. He said his name was Carleton and he worked for the United States Department of Agriculture. "We never know when the rust is coming or where it'll land," he told Nikolai, "but this year it spared the Russian farmers, and they've got a record-breaking harvest." He chewed on a wheat seed. "This is good stuff. Better than ours back home. Tastier. Lighter. Might make good macaroni. I'm taking some seed back with me."

"Are you allowed to do that?" Nikolai asked.

"Why wouldn't I be allowed?" Carleton answered, perplexed.

Saskatchewan. 1918. As far as the horizon, golden wheat. A tall farmer, with a barrel chest and squinty eye, held his son on his shoulder. He turned to Nikolai.

"Tell him, boy," he said.

"It's a new variety. Called Marquis," said the boy. "We shall soon be rich."

Saskatchewan. 1955. Barren black fields belching smoke as the farmers burned the infected crop. "Stem rust," said the grown-up son; barrel chested; squinty eyed; bitter as the smoke. "This land has been in our family for a hundred years. We'll be lucky to sell it for the cost of moving out. We're going to lose everything. So much for blasted Marquis."

Des Moines, Iowa. 1919. Nikolai stood in the back of a church, where a group of women, all of them white-skinned and wearing laced shoes, were attending a lecture by a young man in a three-piece suit.

"Now listen carefully, ladies. This is barberry. This is where the killer rust goes to breed." The speaker held up a picture and a branch. The women leaned in to look. "Barberry has to be eliminated. Every single bush that can be found in the 13 grain states of the USA must be torn out and destroyed. No barberry. No rust." He glared at them. "You must awaken the public to this peril. Organize the people. Tell everyone."

Hibbing, Minnesota. 1920. Nikolai marched with another group of ladies carrying signs that said "Kill the barbarian barberry!"

Lincoln, Nebraska. 1921. A man on a tractor plowed a barberry hedge into a dead heap. Nikolai rummaged through the smashed bushes. Rust covered his fingertips. He pressed 'Zoom.' Then again. And again. Had he seen this leaf before? Maybe a different color? Under a different name? Maybe smaller....

He pressed another button.

Tibet. 1927. A smiling Russian fellow wearing a pale suit, a flowery tie and a fedora was striding toward him, arms outstretched in greeting. "Ah, my dear Tencing," he said. "How good it is to see you." He shook Nikolai's hand and sat down beside him.

Nikolai's throat closed on a gasp. This Russian had called him by the name of his own ancestor! *I must look like him. The face of my family is preserved here in this place.*

"Here's the mystery, old friend," the Russian said. "I have come from Ukraine. Terrible plague on the wheat there. People will go hungry. Of course, a bad situation has been made catastrophic by the stupidity and cruelty of our government, but that is another story.

"Now I have made two trips through these mountains to this village, and I have never seen or heard of this plague here. So if you are agreeable, I would like to buy some of your purple wheat - I believe you call it 'Lucky Boy' - and some of the little white alpine violets that always grow nearby. Name your price, Tencing. I have a suspicion that the flora of your village may save the people of our young Soviet Union from starvation."

The Russian botanist gave Nikolai a cup and took one for himself and filled them with vodka from an embossed silver bottle. Nikolai recognized the bottle. It had occupied a place of honor on his father's mantle.

"To Lucky Boy!" the Russian toasted.

How could he know that all the flora of the natural world would not save the people of the Soviet Union from starvation instigated by the cruelty and stupidity of their government? How could he know that he himself would not be saved?

This is the man I was named for. This great caring man.

Nikolai's eyes filled with tears. He saw everything he had tried to forget. His little sisters giggling as they trailed behind the herd of grazing yaks. His father struck down by the soldiers, bleeding in the dirt. His mother running with Oberon through the blowing barley, screaming at the soldiers who were taking away her boy, screaming his name and reaching up for him as the sunflight lifted off.

He couldn't sit there a minute longer. He raced for the exit, past the eyes of the scanner that stripped him to his bones lest he try to steal anything. The lady called from her desk: "Your food! You forgot your food!"

In the street, gulping air, Nikolai staggered against the AgMuseum wall and pressed his face against the stone, beating his head against the cold stone, trying to clear his mind. He felt sick. He felt exactly as though he had tossed back too much vodka on a bright cold day almost 250 years earlier in Tibet. He smelled it on his hands. It burned his throat and churned in his belly.

He threw up. He kicked dirt over the mess to bury it and finally, overcome with grief, slid to his knees, sobbing.

People who passed assumed he was drunk or crazy and left him alone. But one tall girl came over and crouched down next to him, asking if he was okay, would he like a drink of water, could she give him a hand?

Feeling wretched and embarrassed, Nikolai accepted the water. He drank some and washed his face and hands. The girl helped him to his feet. She smiled.

She had dark blue eyes with very thick lashes, curly light brown hair and light brown skin too. She had soft looking pink lips and wonderful long legs. She was, he thought, incredibly beautiful.

"How sick are you? Do you need a doctor?"

"No. It's just that I have come a long way and have had to go to work immediately upon arriving here and I haven't had much sleep and the food is so different... I had...that is, I thought I had too much to drink. And the air is so thick, the AgMuseum, so closed. Made me feel a bit ill."

 Nikolai doubted that she would be interested in a man with vomit on his shoes who stank of vodka and sat sobbing in a public park, but he gave it a shot anyway.

"My name is Nikolai Juma Das. I am a plant scientist. I am here from the University of the Wind in Mongolia. To study diseases of wheat."

She only smiled. Most likely a proper girl, not accustomed to giving her name to strangers.

But then an older women called to her. "Lizzie! Come back here this minute!" So then he knew.

Lizzie, he thought, watching her butt and her legs as she walked away. Elizabeth. Like the ancient queen who lived at the time of Shakespeare.

6. EMMY hovered in the skies...

*E*MMY hovered in the skies over north central Asia. She was ravenous. The little meal in Mongolia had only piqued her appetite. She wanted more. But she didn't know which way to go.

For thousands of years, her relatives had ignored this part of the world. It was too cold for wheat here, the sky too filled with blizzards, the ground too frozen, nothing to eat. Recently, however, conditions had improved. The earth had warmed up. People were growing wheat in the wind-swept hills now.

Her older sisters had tried the new grains and been repelled by the walls of rejection planted inside them and just died away of starvation. Luckily for EMMY, she had powers those sisters lacked. She was the vengeance of nature, newer than the newest grain, born and bred in a wild European barberry bush, and she could slip past any wall anywhere.

Perhaps she could hitch a ride with one of the puffy little clouds that was sailing west toward Kazakhstan. From there a breeze might blow her on toward Ukraine and Russia. Yum.

Or maybe the fickle winds would blow her eastward, toward China.

Too bad those Chinese agrotechs were always thinking up horrible poisons to make their grains inedible. An itinerant fungus could never know what they were cooking in their gene caldrons. They might stop her before she could find a way to cross the great sea to where she **really** wanted to go -- the lush new hillside fields of northern California.

She sensed that no puffy little cloud would be able to transport her across these distant international boundaries. EMMY needed a big strong 100-mile-an-hour hurricane force gale that would keep *on blowing long enough to allow her to find the moisture and temperate air that she and the wheat loved. And then she would only have to stretch down her long red powdery arms and gorge.*

Well, she would just have to continue hovering in the skies above north central Asia and see what opportunities the winter storms might bring.

7. THE FUNERAL SONG

The death of Great Uncle Clyde changed everything. Grandma's new plan was that we would meet Mom in St. Paul for the funeral and then fly back to Oregon right after I finished singing "Blooming Fields."

"Blooming Fields", author unknown, is rented by the Agroclans Society on a yearly basis for use at their in-house memorials.

> **He (she) wanders now through blooming fields,**
> **No drought or floods beset him (her),**
> **He (she) gave his (her) all to feed us all,**
> **We never shall forget him (her)...**

...and yada yada yada.

Bored as I was by that creepy song, I couldn't afford to show it, because for me, the funeral of this distant relative I had never met was going to be an audition. My singing teacher, Mrs. Lightfinger, had warned me that scouts from the major music schools could be present, and that my performance would determine how much they bid for me at the Music Talent Auction.

The black dress I had brought with me might suit a funeral but not a funeral that was also an audition.

"This is our cue to go shopping!" Grandma enthused. "Let's find you something sad but dressy, dark but glittery. Nice long dangling earrings. And new shoes! Oh, this is going to be a fabulous fun day!"

Grandma believed that a singer must always dress her throat before anything, for that was the part that held the power. So we bought a locket of azure stone on an iron chain, with a secret compartment for a picture or whatever behind the stone. Then we went looking for clothes to dress the rest of me.

We shopped for hours. There was absolutely nothing nice in my size in St. Paul. Nothing.

Never had I hated my body so much as that day. I stood in the middle of Summit Avenue and stamped my ginormous feet and just screamed.

"Why am I the tallest girl in North America?! Why am I cursed?! Look at these people. They are all short. Short short teensy-weensy. What happened to all those Norwegian genes?! And besides, they have terrible taste. No flair. No style. This city is a rural outback, a wasteland. No self-respecting Angelena can possibly find anything to wear in public here."

"Lizzie darling..."

"You sing at the funeral, Grandma. I'm going home!"

"Calm yourself, my love," Grandma said. "I have an idea. I know a Ceil over the Wisconsin border in Webster who runs a specialty shop for men who like to dress up as women, and half of her customers are slender and six feet tall." I howled in protest. "Sorry, darling. Five foot eleven. Just like you."

So off we went on a hoverbus to Ceil's Cross Dresses, with Grandma sparking and me grumping along behind, and wouldn't you know, Grandma was right again.

The Ceil there, a delightful fluttering man, looked at me all over like he was my dermatologist.

"We are seeking the unique, Ceil," Grandma said, "the startling, okay okay, let's be honest, the gaudy. After all, our Lizzie is an entertainer. Everything must be blue or violet to accentuate her eyes. She needs loose sleeves or no sleeves to maximize freedom of movement. Now I am going to sit right here on this bench. Bring us what you have. Dazzle me."

Ceil ordered his two assistants to bring this and that and that and this, piles and piles of clothes, more fancy clothes in my size than I had ever seen before in my life. I felt a little dizzy. So many choices! How could I decide?

"Not to worry, darling," Grandma said. "You're only confused because your fashion allergic mother has not taken you shopping enough. I am here. I shall guide you."

For the funeral, we bought a long dark purple tunic with matching tights. (One of Ceil's assistants let it out in the chest.)

Twinkle lights sparkled on the hem and the sleeves. The neck was cut wide just over my collarbone, framing the azure locket. And there were other outfits too, studded with beads, bordered with metallic embroidery, to wear onstage when I returned to Ashland.

At last I had the gleaming wardrobe of a real entertainer.

We bought a new blue suitcase to hold it all.

My fashion allergic mother, receiving the purchase orders as we shopped, called to rage about the cost.

"May I remind you, Evangeline," Grandma said, "that these outfits are for Lizzie to wear onstage during her forthcoming show at the Ashland Wet Spot, which is comping this entire vacation, making it unnecessary for you and your brother Furlong to foot the bill. So stop complaining and just say thank you."

We were on our way back to our hotel, crossing the square, loaded with packages, when I saw the guy beating his head against the wall of the round red building.

"Look Grandma..." I said.

"A better idea is not to look, darling. That man is drunk and crazy and sick. Don't go near him."

But when he threw up and collapsed and began to cry, I could not help myself. I dropped my packages on the ground and ran over to the poor guy to see if I could help him. I mean, sometimes you've just got to follow your instinct and not be afraid.

How could I have known he would turn out to have such bright black eyes?

Of course, when I pulled him to his feet, the top of his head just about made it to my nose. So I got over the eyes right away. Still, his hand had a sort of warm feeling...

He spoke like a foreigner. I could see he was totally mortified, the way he turned away to wipe his face, the way he tried to explain his behavior and give his credentials. Something about wheat. *God,* I thought. *Another farmer.*

I left my water tube with the foreigner and went off across the square to rejoin Grandma, thinking *He's watching me. I can feel it. He's looking at my legs.*

"That man was sick," Grandma said. "And you got right down into his face. What if you caught something from him, what if you get a cold and cannot sing? For heaven's sake, darling, you have to realize that you must be careful with yourself. Your whole future depends on it."

"He wasn't really sick, Grandma. He's an agrotech who just arrived from overseas and somebody gave him too much to drink and something in our food didn't agree with him, that was all, no biggie." I picked up the packages. "Let's find a hoverbus stop. I can't carry all this stuff back to our hotel."

"Put those down this minute," Grandma said. "Now. Please. Watch. Learn."

She placed her hands on her hips and stood looking down at the big pile of packages with consternation. Then she looked around, her face radiating anxiety. The response was amazing.

A young man stopped to ask if he could give her a hand. An old man leaning on a cane and passing in the other direction asked if he could be of assistance. A red-haired boy giving his girl a ride on his hoverbike flew past. The girl made him turn around and return to Grandma and offer to help. So we set off for our hotel, each of our super nice St. Paulsy friends carrying a couple of packages and Grandma riding where the girl had been riding before.

I glanced back to see if the foreigner was still there, but he had disappeared.

Arliss predicted terrible storms. Many sunflights were grounded. So even though Mom had secured permission as a pertinent attendee, she couldn't make it to the funeral. She felt awful. I mean, how many great uncles did she have? Turned out lots of other people who had been cleared to attend couldn't get there either. To deepen everyone's frustration, the storms didn't happen in the end.

We gathered in Great Uncle Clyde's wheat fields. They had been carved into blocks, each variety of wheat in its own block, the blocks separated by thin stone pathways, regular as a suburb. The grave, already dug and filled with algae logs, had been fitted into the space between the inner corners of blocks 12 and 13, 16 and 17. We stood on the outer edges of these four blocks. Three sides for the mourners. One side for the funeral master – Athena's Professor Felicity Bjornsdottir -- and the funeral singer – that's me – and her accompanist – that's Paco, with his big old 12-string guitar.

"It's a Martin," he explained to the many folks who seemed eager to know. "Present from my dad. He used to say 'Giving you that damn guitar was the dumbest thing I ever done.'"

An audiotech wearing a baby blue sweater (could that be *real* wool?) clipped a little bead to the iron chain of my locket. It was no bigger than a lady bug, but I still felt it ruined my look.

"Please put it someplace hidden," I said.

He tucked it under my bra strap. He was a handsome man, and he smelled nice and clean. He had a really pretty bracelet for his Incoming. "Press this end to be heard by the people," he said. "Press that end if you also want to hear what the people are saying to you."

Felicity needed the assistance of two ordermen to mount the platform. My cousin Athena, who worked with her at The Antarctic Germplasm Bank, had described her to me. I had always figured she was exaggerating until I saw the real thing. Felicity looked like a huge round white tea pot. She had wide round hips and breasts, a moon face ringed by wisps of pale blonde hair that hung in a thick braid way down her back to her apartment-sized behind. She wore a shapeless tent dress of eggshell white, belted under her bosom. Its hem bunched up on the tops of her white boots.

"Athena has told me about you," she said, squeezing my hand. "Her gifted songbird cousin ummm...ummm...sorry sorry sorry...names..."

"Lizzie. And this is my accompanist, Paco El Din."

"I'm sorry really sorry really that I could not bring ummm..."

"Athena."

"She was too badly needed at the germplasm bank in my absence. Will you come and visit us? Perhaps I could import you on an entertainment visa, and you could sing and enliven the long polar nights. Oh boy oh boy, wouldn't we all enjoy that!" She looked up at the gathering crowd. "So many peo-peo-peo... What if I forget what to sssss...?"

"I believe you have your speech right there on your Incoming, ma'am," Paco said. "All you have to do is read it."

"Oh yes, here it is. What a relief. I forgot that I wrote it down so I wouldn't have to remember it."

Hundreds of people were arriving, generations of Clyde Bright's students and colleagues, many of them already in tears. The Caliph had sent a delegation. So had the Chinese Emperor. Even some minor powers, like the Mongols, were represented.

The crowd parted as Great Uncle Clyde's body was rolled in, encased in a clear optical shield. Three men were pushing it A downcast, round-shouldered man wearing boots and a battered cowboy hat. A tall, gaunt gentleman, dressed in flowing sand-colored clothing. "Stevie and Itamar. I love these guys," said Professor Bjornsdottir. "They tried so hard to get me pregnant. The other one, that'sthat'sthat's ummmm..."

We didn't know who he was. We couldn't help her. She turned red and swelled and looked like she was going to burst open. But then...

"Jedda! Yes yes our Corporate boss man, Horatio Jedda. He has never before made a public appearance. In case you did not realize what an important man your umm ummm..."

"Great Uncle Clyde."

"....your Great Uncle Clyde was, here is your proof."

We waited for an extra half an hour to give the crowd time to assemble. I had never seen so many people physically face-to-face in one place. I'll bet there were at least 200! If you added all the people like Mom who wanted to come and couldn't because of Arliss' storm warning, there probably would have been hundreds more.

On a signal from a scary-looking woman, they lowered Great Uncle Clyde's body into the pit.

Felicity Bjornsdottir read her speech without a hitch.

"Clyde Bright was our teacher," she said. "Our beloved guide in life. The man who chose us and gave us a chance to work with him and learn from him. We who came from The Generation of Famine, born into a starving world, he fed us on hope for its rescue. We who came from The Generation of War, raised on violence and tragedy, he gave us the gift of a future. He was our fountain in the drought. Our sunbeam in the deluge. Let us bury him here in the garden of his creation, so his ashes

s can do what he did during his life - nourish the rebirth of our exhausted planet."

Paco played the opening chords of "Blooming Fields." I started to sing. Then I stopped.

I looked into Paco's eyes. Shook my head. His hands fell silent on the strings. He waited. The crowd waited.

I knew I had to change the song.

Maybe it was because there were so many people.

I had this feeling that somehow it wasn't right to sing *to* them, that I needed a song that would allow them to sing *along*, so they would feel like they were participating in Great Uncle Clyde's life and work, so they would feel encouraged and leave the funeral with hope, the way Professor Bjornsdottir said Clyde had given her hope.

And maybe it was because I felt so important, so in control, wearing my beautiful new outfit, with the Corporate executive there rolling my great uncle to his grave, imagining all the music scouts hiding in the throng, waiting for something that would knock their socks off.

I whispered to Paco: "'That Land of Once'. G-major. Slow."

Sometimes you just have to follow your instinct and not be afraid.

I sang how that land had once been our country, coast-to-coast, even though half of each coast now lay far beneath the swamping sea. I sang the song slower than it is meant to be sung so that people could learn it and join in. On the chorus reprieve, I called out each line and then waited for the people to sing it with me before calling out the next line.

Where had I learned to do that? Oh right. From one of those historic interactives at Grandma's restaurant. An old guy who played the banjo sang the song that way, one line from him, the same line from the audience. I watched him. I sang along with him. He taught me.

I saw Grandma in the crowd, standing among the St. Paulsy folks who had carried our packages. She blew me a kiss.

I saw Nikolai Juma Das.

And then all the people were singing. It felt like even the wheat was singing. The crowd swayed. Strangers took the hands of strangers. Harmony happened. *Hundreds of people were singing because I had taught them the song.* God, what a high that was!

Paco nudged me. We couldn't help but notice that one woman had her back turned to us. She wasn't singing it all. She was giving directions to a bunch of ordermen. Her floppity arms flapped. With the song heading for its refrain, I called: "Sing along, everybody! Come on, Sally, you too, sing along!"

Sally turned and glared. Paco and I smiled and waved, like we were idiots and had not figured out by now that she was Major Sally Kim Lee of the Continental Ordermen Corps, attached to the vacation of Foxie Burton Bright and her granddaughter.

The song ended. The tall woman clicked off the optical shield and lit the fire and Uncle Clyde was consumed. All you could hear was the crackle of the flames and the sound of people weeping.

The mourners at the edge of the crowd started to leave. Paco and I helped Dr. Bjornsdottir climb down from our little stage. But we found that it was impossible to reach Grandma because we were surrounded by shareholders clamoring to speak to us. I remembered the audiotech with the blue sweater and pressed the lady bug under my bra strap so I could hear what the people were saying.

You were wonderful! they said. *I remember that song. My grandmother sang it to me with a little bit different lyrics when I was a kid. And that guitar! Sounded so beautiful... Will you come and sing for us at our harvest party?...For my daughter's wedding?...For the winter holidays? How can we reach you?*

They began to call us by name as though we were friends.

You know in the old days, Lizzie, before you and Paco were born, people could take pictures of events like this and put them on the old public web and share them... Oh please...I swear, it's true!... Don't pay any attention to him, Lizzie, he always exaggerates to make the story better....Please, Lizzie, tell us how we can find out where you are appearing....I'll never forget this day. It was so sad. But I haven't felt this heart warmish in years. Thank you, Lizzie! Thank you, Paco! Thank you!

They pressed in tighter and tighter.

I loved them.

Really, I wanted to hug them all.

At the same time I was afraid of them, afraid they would squeeze us to death, but oh, I loved them so much.

Paco tried to protect us. He pulled me close to him. His guitar in its heavy case hung across his back and banged against my shoulders. The crowd spilled out around us. People were asking me questions, seeking my personal opinion.

So Lizzie, tell us, who do you think will replace Dr. Bright? I think maybe Professor Foster.... Foster?! Are you kidding? Did you see him? He looked terrible. Must be sick. .... What do you think of Mugombo, Lizzie?... God I hope they don't pick him. I had him for Brassicas and Legumes. He was such a nut. He kept trying to get us to talk to the plants... Maybe they'll pick Professor Bjornsdottir.

Wouldn't that be just grand, Lizzie? Don't you just love her? I don't think they ought to leave her freezing down south in that snowsy seed vault. What do you think?

Women reached out to touch the material of my tunic. *Where did you get that gorgeous outfit? Did you have it made special? I love the glitter.*

They put messages in Paco's pockets. I swear it's true. Girls and boys too, they actually whispered their information onto discs and slipped the discs into the pockets of his jeans. I mean, talk about brazen.

A short man with a big black moustache and blackout goggles and a wide brimmed hat gave me a bone-crushing hug and whispered that I was even more terrific than Grandma had said I was and he was so proud of me, I was the big surprise bonus of his old age.

I heard a whining sound. Paco heard it too. I threw myself and Grandpa to the ground. Paco whirled around and a bullet from nowhere smashed into the guitar case. Grandpa crawled away into the crowd and disappeared. Paco was screaming. So was I. So was everybody.

They tried to shoot Lizzie! They almost killed Paco! They shot his guitar!

This message tore through the crowd like a runaway hoverbus.

Major Sally Kim Lee and her ordermen did not move.

Twenty people lifted me and Paco high on their shoulders to show the crowd that we were okay.

Then the sky turned dark.

A horrible chirping noise filled the heavens.

A lady behind me cried out that it was the minions of Satan come to punish us for our sins.

Paco told her not to be concerned, it was probably just a plague of locusts. Turned out it was a ginormous herd of swallows.

Then we had snow. One of the flakes landed on my azure locket. Actually the flake was a little piece of real paper. The swallow herds flew off. The chirping stopped. Daylight returned.

Read it to us, Lizzie! somebody yelled. *What does it say?*

Sitting on the shoulders of our fans, I turned the lady bug up high and read the paper out loud.

"It says 'Weather Report from Eddie Bright, the Farmer's Friend'." Everybody was either listening or reading along on their own copy, for thousands had descended from the wings of the over-flying swallows. "Clear skies and temperatures in the mid-80s will continue for the rest of this week from the Mississippi to the Rockies. The western hills will have temps in the 70s and light rain every other night throughout the growing season. Can't ask for better. But there's a severe heat wave descending on Central Asia. Kazakhstan's wheat and forage could take a big yield hit. Emergency imports will be needed. West coast farmers should plant from fence post to fence post.

"Professor Clyde Bright of Nebraska was a North American hero. Keep him in your hearts. Continue his work."

8. POPULAR MUSIC

The appalling incident at Clyde Bright's funeral had made Horatio Jedda very angry. In all his years with the Corporation, he had never been forced to deal with the issue of popular music (compared to which, he thought, agrotech was a piece of cake.) Now, the music and the musicians had plunged into the center of his story – and all because some idiot had tried to assassinate Eddie Bright.

Ever since Clyde's death, Horatio had been sending conciliatory messages to Eddie.

"The hell with those wartime broadcasts. All is forgiven. The Corporation understands. You had a daughter and a son-in-law at the front. You were panicked as any father might be, looking for someone to blame. We understand. Let's forget it. Come home.

"The old satellites are just space junk. Everyone can see them falling out of orbit. We depend completely on our weather people now. Arliss can't handle this. He's basically just an entertainer. We need an historian, a statistical plotter, a pattern-seer. We need you, Eddie. Come home. Be one of us again."

The Farmer's Friend would not answer.

He slipped silently from hideout to hideout. He seemed to have the impression that Horatio was trying to kill him. A paranoid old fool, Horatio thought, slaughtering a benign little bird spy in a fit of panic.

Horatio kept after him.

"Find me after Clyde's funeral. We'll go out to 'Rose'n'Harry's' and eat some real steak. I'll make you an offer. Believe me, I can be very generous. Get your freedom back, Eddie. Your beautiful wife. Your home. Your peace of mind."

But then a sub-set of envy-ridden thugs in the Meteorology Department had screwed up everything. They went rogue and hired an assassin to kill Eddie Bright with a drone gun and an unmarked bullet, justifying the old man's paranoia, undoubtedly confirming him in his determination to stay underground. Stupid stupid stupid. Not only had they missed their target. They had destroyed, according to the hysterical director of the Orchestra Coalition, one of the four 12-string Martin classical guitars remaining in the entire world. And worst of all, they had created just what the Entertainment Division had always warned about — young musical stars with an independent fan base.

So outraged was the crowd at the apparent attack on Lizzie Corelli and Paco El Din that Major Sally had been forced to order her troops to stand down, a strategy lost on no one. An unknown Turkish hacker felt encouraged enough to crack every international audiovisual safecode and record the incident and drop it onto The Beam right in the middle of the cooking show.

The Chairman blew his stack. He called an emergency meeting of the International Affairs Division. The diplomats reported that New Ottomon Orbit emissaries had denied all knowledge of the hacker, and it appeared they were telling the truth. *Some troublesome brainiac just showing off, sir. Let the Turks take care of him.*

The Chairman calmed down.

Internal Order quickly caught the failed assassin. She was questioned. Who had hired her? Who had spotted Eddie for her? Who had given her the code to the drone gun? After one long night, the ordermen had their answers.

The leaders of the plot were rounded up. Arliss testified against them at the brief private trial, red-faced with shame that such low-life should have infiltrated the Meteorology Department.

The verdict was "Guilty" and the sentence was "Disappearance."

Usually in such cases, Horatio sent an appeal for clemency, and because of the respect in which he was held, it was often heeded. "We're a company not a tyranny," he would say. "We depend on the good will of our shareholders. We can't allow ourselves to get a reputation for political murder."

This time, he made no such appeal.

At a moment when the Agrotech Division was trying to deal with the potential destruction of the whole world's wheat crop, and nothing was more important than an accurate weather report, they had tried to kill North America's best weatherman. They deserved to die.

As for the singing kids, Lizzie and Paco, well, they would have to be disciplined.

In Horatio's philosophy, kids always posed a danger. Not only did they behave irrationally, they caused others to do so as well. Look at the ridiculous risk Eddie Bright had run just to see his granddaughter perform. Most disturbing, concern for kids could trigger a disturbing downtrend in the standard of sufficiency. "You always want more for your children," his own hard-working father had said.

For these reasons, Horatio generally tried to hire the childless. This was not a difficult thing to do. The advances in medical technology may have lengthened life, but they had not been able to increase it. The fertility of the whole population – people and animals and plants alike -- had plummeted. The pollutants of the past, now outlawed, had crept into the genetic heritage of the living. Genes didn't develop. Or they didn't do the job originally intended for them. Babies were born sick, if they lived to be born at all. Among women, pregnancy was the second highest cause of death after suicide. The debates about reproductive rights, which had so disturbed ancient generations, seemed like little blasts of pointless rhetoric now. In the 22nd century, abortion to save the mother's life had become a civic obligation.

Agrotechs were particularly exposed to seed-snuffing chemicals and rays, so they had even fewer babies than the rest of the people. However, the will to leave progeny behind could still surface, a Darwinian imperative. Jedda watched The Grain Guardians for any signs of surrogate children.

Itamar Mugombo had lots of young assistants who helped him search the desert for bits of microbial detritus that might be coaxed to grow into living plants. Jedda's spymaster, Esmerelda Wolf, reported that they came and went constantly. No special cases.

The seed librarian, Felicity, had always lived lonely, until a few years before when her male colleagues had made a collective attempt to get her pregnant.

Working quietly through the genetics lab networks, Stevie Foster and Itamar Mugombo had come up with a combined sperm cocktail, hoping that one of the little critters might catch up with a Bjornsdottir ovum and give all three of them a real living baby to call their own.

They tried and tried. It didn't work. It never even started to work.

Felicity descended into a terrible depression. Horatio was forced to have her locked up for a full year in a Corporate recovery center. Then one day, as if by a miracle, she was her own sweet self again. Bursting with ideas. Stuttering, yes. Seriously overweight, yes. But still absolutely a genius.

Horatio watched her every move for many months before returning her to work. She had developed some problems with short term memory. When she was upset, coherent speech deserted her. However, with the help of her assistant, Athena Burton, she was doing a better job than ever running the germplasm bank.

Athena Burton. Certainly a surrogate daughter figure in Felicity's life. She could be a problem. Her father was a major wheat grower. Her mother headed the influential ladies' auxiliary of the Northern California Agroclans Society. Her grandmother was Eddie Bright's ex-wife, Foxie. Horatio would have to move carefully with Athena.

The Himalayan kid, Nikolai Juma Das, so devoted to Stevie Foster, had no such protective advantages.

"He has the build of a courier," Horatio said to Esmerelda. "Find some reason to get rid of him."

"I have been ordered to send you away," Stevie said. "For security reasons. Mrs. Wolf is scared that since you worked in China, you may feel loyal to the Empire and give up the secrets of our research."

Nikolai burst out laughing, recalling his days as a slave laborer on the Chinese coast.

"Any place you've been hankering to go?" Stevie continued. "I could get you a visa for rest and rehab."

"I would like to go home."

Stevie was surprised. "I thought you wanted to stay away."

"I do. I cannot bear the thought of seeing my village drowned in mud. But when I was in the AgMuseum, I saw one of my own ancestors. It was 1927. He was drinking vodka with the Russian botanist for whom I am named. They were friends, Professor Foster. Dr. Vavilov was buying some of the old-fashioned purple wheat our family grew in those days. I saw the silver flask he gave my ancestor. It used to live on the mantle, a treasure in our house. All my memories came back to me and they do not leave me alone any more. I have to return home, sir. I have to go and look for the bones of my family."

In short order, Nikolai had a personal tragedy visa and a ticket on the evening sunflight to Lhasa. With a few hours to himself before boarding, he decided to break the law.

He slipped down a side street where thickets of pale purple lilacs grew, and with his exquisitely sharp knife, he cut a big bunch. He knew full well that the penalty for cutting a living plant without authorization could be six months of hard labor on someone's farm. But the memory of Lizzie's face, blazing with excitement and confidence, her song soaring out to the crowd, uniting the people, making them love one another, the memory of that performance tore at his heart. The bullet that killed the guitar could have killed her. She would have been gone forever and would never know how greatly he admired her.

He had to see her.

He learned the name of her hotel from some people who had been standing near her grandmother at the funeral.

He wrapped the lilacs with a corn silk string. Looked like a delivery boy. Felt like a fool. He made it down the hallways to her room and with every step, he wanted to run away.

She was too tall for him. Too talented. Too well-connected. Her accompanist was taller than she, good-looking, unbelievably expert at playing that big guitar, and probably he was her boyfriend. Men who heard her sing must constantly beseech her with their desires.

She won't remember me. She'll laugh in my face. I ought to leave here at once, he thought, ringing the bell.

Her grandmother answered the door, looking enraged. "What the hell do you want?" she snapped.

"Uh...I uh...Lizzie?"

"LIZZIE!" shrieked the grandmother, turning away from him. "You can come out of the bathroom now. Someone is delivering flowers."

She came crashing out of the bathroom, slamming the door behind her, hissing at her grandmother: "I hate you, I hate you, you have ruined my life!" and stopped just short of the lilacs. She was wearing a bathrobe. Her face was bleary with tears. Her hair was wet. "Oh my God," she said when she saw him. She clutched together the lapels of her robe, making Nikolai think that maybe she was naked underneath.

He stepped back, away from her. Thrust the lilacs into her hands.

"These are for you," he said. "You are wonderful. A great talent. So these are for you."

She bit back her tears and smiled at him. "Thank you," she said. "They're beautiful."

"I am going away for a while," he said. "To my old home in the far mountains. Will you be here when I get back?"

"I don't know where I will be. I have just had some terrible news. The Music Talent Auction reviewed my credentials and...and...and nobody bid on me. Because my grandfather...because I am politically undesirable. So I am now without a future as a singer. No conservatory, no teachers, no extra octave, nothing." Tears came pouring again. Her nose dripped. "I'm sorry. You shouldn't have to see me like this."

"You saw me when I was throwing up at the AgMuseum."

She sniffed. "That's true," she said. She smiled. "I love these flowers. Thank you. They are just what I needed."

"Well. Good luck to you," Nikolai said. He walked back down the hall a little way, then changed his mind and returned to the doorway. She was still standing there, no longer clutching her robe, her face in the lilacs.

"I too had a plan for my life," he offered. "An army came and took it away. So I made a new plan. And look, here I am in your country at your door. What matters is the spirit you have inside you. Here." He held his fist against his chest. "You have the voice. You have the power. You had the courage to sing what you knew those people needed to hear. So it makes no difference if they don't let you go to school. The audience is your school. If they kill you, yes, that is the end. But as long as you are alive and singing, you own your own future."

He bent and kissed her hand, and in a sudden rush of deep feeling, turned it over and kissed the palm, pressed the palm of her hand against his face.

"I live in NewLA," she said. "You can always reach me at my mother's antique store. It's called 'The Past on Pico Two.'"

"Well then, perhaps we shall chance to see each other again."

"I hope so," she said. "Safe journey."

Then he left. Once in the long hall, he turned and looked back. She raised her kissed palm.

9. PAYBACK

No sooner had the funeral ended than my big moment in the spotlight began to crash and burn.

Grandma and I had returned to our hotel, to pack up for the trip back to Oregon. I had never seen her so excited. My success had fulfilled her dreams. She was sort of glowing. Me, I just felt empty; collapsed; like my bones had been sucked out by the crowd. The babble of the people, their hands their faces the *push* of them, it was all a big blurred frenzy now. I couldn't remember anything clearly except the whine of the bullet and the death of Paco's guitar, how it hummed and twanged and vibrated for minutes after being hit.

Had Grandpa really been there? Was it really him in that silly disguise? What was that itch on my shoulder? Oh, the lady bug amplifier. Why hadn't the audiotech taken it back?

I stashed the lady bug inside my azure locket and tucked the locket deep into the toe of my boot, went into the bathroom, stripped off my sweat-drenched clothes and stood in the sudsy mist for the whole 120 seconds that is allowed. Then Grandma called to me: "Don't come out of there naked, Lizzie. We have visitors." So I put on my robe.

A burly young orderman had entered our room. When he saw me, he cleared his throat and smiled. He was missing some teeth. Maybe a former wrestler, I thought, or a hockey player. He seemed like a nice guy. They often do actually, seem like nice guys.

"Elizabeth Corelli?"

"Yes, that's me."

"Got this message to give you." He cleared his throat. "'Attention Elizabeth Corelli. Your qualifications were reviewed at the Music Talent Auction. You were found to be unacceptable, so no one bid on you. You have been passed over. Your name has been removed from the list of qualified candidates.' Please acknowledge that you have received this message."

Grandma screamed and reached for me.

"Don't touch me," I said.

The orderman held his Outgoing up to my face. "You are supposed to say *Yes. I have received the message. Thank you.*"

"Asshole!" Grandma hissed.

"That was not the voice of Elizabeth," he told his Outgoing.

"Was my accompanist bid on?" I asked.

"Mr. Paco El Din's family withdrew his name from consideration and took him back to North Carolina. Please acknowledge receipt."

"I have received the message," I said.

"You're supposed to say thank you," he said.

"And you're supposed to be a human being, you sniveling shit!" raged Grandma. She looked like a mad dog. Her upper lip had withdrawn and all her perfect white teeth were sticking out. "How dare you break this young girl's heart and then demand that she say thank you?!"

"It's the accepted form," he said.

He told his Outgoing that, for the record, Elizabeth had refused to say thank you. Then he left.

We stood in silence. I mean, after all, what could be said? Grandma was the first to try.

"Lizzie darling, listen…"

"Don't *Lizzie darling* me, Grandma. This is your fault."

"Lizzie…"

"You have sucked me into something I don't even understand, you have filled me with ideas I never dreamed of having, and now my whole life is ruined."

"Oh sweetheart…."

"Nobody even bid on me! Passed over. Paaaaassssed over! And it's all because Eddie Son-of-a-bitch Bright is my Grandpa!"

"Lower your voice, young lady. Grandpa and I have never had anything but your best interests at heart."

"All you have at heart is your own ambition, you narcissistic meddler."

That really got her.

"Me narcissistic? ME?! Who threw a pop diva hissy fit because she simply couldn't find a single thing to wear in the entire city of St. Paul? Who decided to change an established, paid-for program at the very last minute on a whim? A personal whim of yours and no one else's, Lizzie." I slammed back into the bathroom and locked the door. Grandma beat on it. "Stop being naïve. Can't you see, this is just some psychological trick by the Corporation? To make you afraid. And turn you against Grandpa. And get you to abandon your own best instincts."

"LEAVE ME ALONE!" I yelled.

And then Nikolai Juma Das showed up with a big bunch of lilacs.

After he left, I went to sleep with the flowers. Grandma was not there when I woke. I lay cuddled in my robe, trying to figure out how I had gotten myself into such a mess.

Grandma's so-called divorce from Eddie Bright was obviously a fabrication to fool the authorities and take the heat off our family. In fact Grandma and Eddie had never stopped being lovers, stealing every moment they could together.

Mom must be in on it too.

Oh my God! That was why she and Uncle Furlong had supported the vacation plan in the first place. To get Grandma out to some wilderness where she could meet up with Eddie.

What a monstrous betrayal, to take a totally innocent, apolitical girl and use her as a façade behind which sexual hanksy panksy and illegal weather reports could be hatched in secret!

Well, all right, maybe not so totally innocent.

I mean, why had I not wondered why ordermen were canoeing down the river with us? Why had I warned Grandpa about Major Sally Kim Lee with those trumped up lyrics by the shore? Why had I pretended that Paco was just an accompanist when he was obviously also our body guard?

Why had I changed the song?

Grandma had it right. It was a whim; an impulse; a thing I had done on my own that had led to disaster. I had chosen, without thinking of the fallout, a song that could easily be regarded as incendiary, and I had involved a whole huge crowd of unsuspecting shareholders in its singing. How could I have been proud of that? Excited by that? *Oh why oh why had I agreed to read the weather report?*

I knew that drone bullet was meant not for me or Paco or the poor guitar but for Grandpa. Why did I throw him to the ground when I heard it coming? Affection? Family loyalty? I thought all I wanted was to go to music school and have glittery clothes and a boyfriend who was tall enough to make me feel good.

Was it possible that I also wanted to own my whole self?

Grandma entered the room and turned on the light. She was carrying a tray with a big bowl of tomato soup.

"Are those real tomatoes in there?" I asked.

"They said so. But they may not know what real is any more."

"Like me."

"Yes."

"I'm sorry, Grandma. I didn't mean anything I said. I was just being a self-centered dumb fool. You were right. I should always listen to you. I love you."

"You are my treasure," she answered, kissing me. "I love you too. Never forget that."

We sat for a few minutes on the bed, just hugging each other.

The desk clerk told me that Paco had left in the middle of the night in the company of his father, a Southern gentleman with a bushy beard, who arrived with two gladiators and physically transported Paco out of the building and put him in a private hoverride and flew away.

I called Paco's Incoming. No answer. I called his family's farm. His mother appeared on the screen. She was a petitesy, prettyish lady, wearing an apron over her pinafore.

"Now listen up, you cheap California hippie bitch," she said. "You are done with my boy, you hear me? You and your strumpet grandmother, you have brought my Paco to the brink of destruction. He could have been killed, and why? Because he was on stage with the granddaughter of a wanted terrorist. So you have seen the back of my Paco, understand? And if you ever try to put your grotesquely tall self in his way again, I will not wait for the dumbass screw-ups at the Meteorology Department. I will personally - me personally, you hear? - have you killed."

The screen went blank.

I leaned on Grandma. She stroked my hair. "So. The Meteorology Department," she murmured thoughtfully. "Okay okay."

After that, they lost my new suitcase.

I mean, they *said* they lost it.

All my glitzy, lit up, show biz clothing just disappeared.

The Corporate "Lost and Found" officer said she would put a tracer on it.

She was standing in front of a ginormous wall of lost suitcases. I could clearly see mine on the third shelf.

"No need for a tracer," I said, pointing. "There it is."

She did not turn to look. "That's not yours," she said.

"Yes, it is. It is. It's a brand new blue suitcase from a store called Oxter's in Minneapolis. I just bought it. Look, my name is on the tag. Lizzie Corelli, that's me."

"We know exactly who you are," she said. "That is not your suitcase. Your suitcase is lost. A tracer will be placed on it. When and if it is found, we will be in touch with you."

"That's my suitcase!" I shouted. "Right there. Why are you stealing it? What do you want with my clothes? They are too big for everyone. Except me."

"Are you creating a disturbance?" she asked.

"You bet I am." I leapt up on the counter, shoved her aside and reached for the suitcase. Mighty arms hauled me down. A couple of them belonged to the bad news orderman with the missing teeth.

"Is this the one who called you a sniveling shit?" asked his friend.

"No, it was the grandmother."

The friend felt me all over to find the weapon he knew damn well I did not have.

"Don't do that," said my hated messenger. "That's not right."

Something in his tone made the groper let me go.

I took one last look at the bulging blue suitcase and staggered away.

So now I had no accompanist.

And nothing to wear except my long black and my short blue. How the hell was I going to bring off a nightly performance at The Ashland Wet Spot?

Turned out that I worried for nothing.

When Grandma and I arrived back at the spa, the first thing we saw was a big sign in the lobby that said TONIGHT! 8 PM IN THE RIVER ROOM. DOWN MEMORY LANE WITH LIZZIE CORELLI. and beneath it a life-size picture of me and across the whole thing a big red banner that screamed CANCELED!

Old folks and gladiators gathered around us in the lobby. They had all bought tickets, they had all received their money back, and they were all terribly disappointed. To our astonishment, some of them had actually seen the funeral on The Beam sewing show, thanks to some no-name Turkish hacker.

One old man said it was a damn disgrace, a crazy renegade shooting into a crowd of mourners and then the ordermen doing zip zero zilch nada to find him or her or whoever. Obviously the ordermen had lost control. The Chairman needed to clean house. Somebody should instigate a purge like they used to have when he was a kid in Uzbekistan.

A teensy lady with a lapful of crocheting told him to get stuffed. "We live in a Corporate democracy here, buddy," she said. "We don't go killing people just because they disagree with us."

This was followed by a little silence.

Our vacation had come crashing to an end. Failure. A total wipeout. Nothing to do but go home.

Three people had brought guitars to replace the one which had been shot. I started to explain that I wouldn't be able to give Paco the guitars because his mother would never let me see him again. Grandma stopped me. "You never know," she said. So we took the guitars.

We settled ourselves into our hoverride, among Grandma's six bags and my one and now the three gift guitars too. It was almost midnight. We were having a big storm. Driving wind. Thunder. Sometimes lightning hit the trees, setting them on fire. But the fires died fast in the pouring rain.

Two hours out of The Ashland Wet Spot, over the New Dead Sea, we ran into the monster bird again. He dropped his latest screaming rat into the roiling, white-capped waters. It was hard to see, but I thought I saw the rat not dissolving but actually swimming free.

Grandma assured me that could not possibly be the case.

In another hour, the hover stopped. When I asked why, it answered that the weather made continued travel too dangerous. The hover settled us onto a rocky ledge. Its storm shield opened like a big tent over us to keep us from getting hit by lightning, and all in all we were pretty cozy.

"It used to be that we looked forward to rain in the spring," Grandma said. "We had a song...about rain showers in April bringing blue birds and daffodils..."

"What're they?"

"Flowers."

"Were they good to eat?"

"I don't know, my darling. We didn't eat them. We just looked at them because they were so beautiful."

I knew she was going to cry, and then I would cry, and what use was that? So I asked her to teach me the song. I tuned up one of the guitars and with the thunder and the wind and the flash fires all around us, Grandma and I sang "The Rains of April" together until I knew it cold. Finally we fell asleep.

I was awakened by somebody tapping on the window.

A little man was standing out there, shouting "Arising, Mademoiselle!" He had bulging eyes and gold rings in his nose and ears. On his narrow back he carried a flute, a trumpet and a trombone. *"Ouvrez la porte, pour l'amour de Dieu!* I am to being so wetness!"

I knew Grandma would say that I shouldn't let a perfect stranger into our hover in a dark and storm-tossed forest in the dead of night, but she was snoring, and this guy was maybe three feet tall. So I let him in.

He shook the rain off himself and cleared his throat. "Mademoiselle! I am having the honor to being Willy Sachertorte, from the drown-ed island of Haiti, for 50 years flutist in the Koncertgebau Orchestra of the drown-ed city of Amsterdam, *votre sauveur ce soir!* We must to going now. *Allons y!"*

"Are you crazy? Who the hell do you think you are? I'm not leaving my grandmother..."

"Not to worry, darling," Grandma stretched. Her joints clicked into place. She slapped herself in the face to wake up properly. "Lovely to see you, Willy dearest." Grandma and Willy gave each other several kisses on both cheeks. "Willy is an old friend of your grandfather's, Lizzie. Go with him. He will take you to safety. He will be your music school."

"But I can't just leave you here."

"And I wish I could go with you, darling, oh how I wish. But I have appearances to keep up. A new cook to hire. Your mother to mollify."

A red-haired boy who looked familiar showed up and began unloading my suitcase and the three guitars. He said "Everything will be fine, Lizzie. I'll make sure Mrs. Burton Bright gets safely home."

"I remember you," I said. "You were riding the hoverbike with your girlfriend in St. Paul. What are you doing here?"

"After I met you and your Grandma and heard you sing and read the weather report of The Farmer's Friend, I joined."

"Joined what?" I asked.

But of course, I already knew.

10. JOINING EDDIE BRIGHT

LE TALL BAND

The trek to Eddie's camp took three days. That whole time, it never stopped raining. Willy Sachertorte led the way, with his brass horns clanking. I carried my suitcase and the three guitars.

Willy was a friend of Grandpa's from the famine times. After Haiti sank and Amsterdam turned into a soggy bog, he decided to look for a higher position and became a food drop pilot. He fought alongside Grandpa in the revolution that brought the Corporation to power. But when the Corporation started telling him which music he could and could not play, Willy bolted and joined Grandpa on the renegade fringe.

"Nobody is owning Willy," he declared. "Willy is playing *quand il veut et comme il veut*, and if he want, for free."

No drone bullet had ever gone looking for Willy, because he was just a three-foot flutist after all, and how dangerous could he be?

At our first dawn, we entered a forest of little white trees. A big sign said:

THIS FOREST WAS PLANTED IN 2157 TO COMMEMORATE THE DAY WHEN THE CHAIRMAN BECAME CHAIRMAN OF THE BOARD. REMOVING ANY PART OF ANY TREE HERE, INCLUDING FALLEN BRANCHES AND/OR LEAVES, IS A CRIME AGAINST THE CORPORATION AND ALL ITS SHAREHOLDERS. VIOLATORS WILL BE SEIZED.

"Is it not strange, *cherie*, that the Chairman has been to leading *l'amerique du nord depuis neuf ans* and never we have seen him?"

Willy did not expect an answer. He was just floating an idea. He does that a lot.

The Chairman's Forest shook constantly beneath our feet. Willy said that was because mining had once been done here, and pipe had once been laid here, and even though all such deep digging had been outlawed since forever, the wounds in the ground had not healed. The whole area had the shakes.

Willy led me through the trees, zigging and zagging. He had everything we needed except sunshine. He had green balls, which blew up into tents to keep us dry. He had crackers, dehydrated veggies and grapesies, fauxburger strips and fresh nutri-water in tubes, all pre-measured in exactly the right amounts required for us to stay okay. He had four waterproofing guns that he used to spray the instruments and protect them. As for us, we pretty much stayed wet.

I was getting tired, but he wasn't, and he was half my size, so I was ashamed to say how tired I was and kept plodding on. It rained and rained. I got really really tired. Just as I was deciding to dump the bravado and demand a rest, Willy collapsed from exhaustion.

We blew up a tent for shelter. I thought maybe one of us should sleep while the other kept watch, but what good would that have done if we were captured by the ordermen? Sleeping or waking, they would have carried us away. So we both settled down and went to sleep.

The drum woke us.

It was getting closer and closer, louder and louder. Big squishy footsteps. The scrawny trees trembled.

Willy grabbed my hand. "Ah, *tout perdu*," he said sadly.

Sunshine Gomez poked his large shaggy head into the tent and whimpered: "Gee, I have been so wet and lonely waiting for you guys."

We took him in and patted him dry.

I had not seen Sunshine since our first night at the Ashland Wet Spot when he fell in love with Grandma and started playing his Armenian drum. But you can bet I remembered him vividly. Taller than me. Huge in the shoulders. And draped with medals for winning the heavyweight wrestling title again and again and again.

He took over carrying my suitcase and Willy's horns and Willy too. I fell in behind them with the three guitars. It was great to have Sunshine with us, but on the other hand, it also made it more likely that the ordermen would come after us. I mean, a profitable athlete can't just overstay his home leave and fail to return to gladiator training camp and not expect to be missed by the people who own 85% of him.

Sunshine explained that for some time now, he had been deliberately losing his matches, complaining of torn tendons, exhibiting flu-like symptoms, hoping that the authorities would actually welcome his defection. Maybe his strategy had worked. As yet no one seemed to be following.

"Ah *pauvre monstre*," laughed Willy, riding high, "perhaps this is to being their strategy not yours. Perhaps they wait to seeing where you will to leading them."

It continued raining. We continued walking. Many of the trees had begun to fall down. I guess nine years is young for a tree, and the roots must have been shallow, and all that battering water must have loosened the soil and *pow!* over we go.

"Too bad about the Chairman's forest," I commented, as we stepped through the tangle of fallen branches.

"*Ce foret ici* is to planting three times *depuis ces neuf ans*," Willy said. "*Trois fois, mes enfants.* Is it not strange that the trees keep to falling down?"

"Maybe the earth is too weak to grow the forest any more," I said.

"*Exactement, cherie.* Once to destroying, not so easy to rebuilding."

By the third day of our trek, my feet were erupting with blisters, my back was aching from guitars, and it was still raining. I wondered whether, if I raised my head to the sky and opened my mouth, I could almost drown myself and pass out and rest in the mud for a while. I was beginning to hallucinate that somebody was playing the Mendelsohn violin concerto.

Then Paco, playing like an angel, descended through the clouds, totally dry in his waterproof flight suit. We disconnected him from his lowering straps, which zipped right back up to the invisible suncopter that had delivered him.

"Hey there, gang," Paco said. "Got some great stuff for us."

He had brought an antique oud, decorated all over with pearlsies and little chips of wood arranged in complicated geometrics, and a brand new state-of-the- art 2167 model Natura Myriada keyboard, which can give you every known musical instrument and up to 400 voices in all ranges, solo and together and in all combinations between, plus *15 different kinds of bird song and both alto and basso frogs! Yayyy!* (The only thing the miracle keyboard can't give you is drums. Even after centuries of trying, the audiotechs have just never been able to replicate the sound and feel of live drums.)

Paco also had his violin, his banjo, and a real original Roma tambourine for me. He had dyed his hair (including his chest hair) lemon yellow.

"How did you get away from your ferocious mother?" I cried. "Where did you get that super keyboard? Who lowered you down from the sky? Why did you dye your hair that horrible color?"

"Not gonna tell you, Miss Lizzie. Because what you don't know can't be beat out of you if you're captured."

Sometimes he is so overdramatic.

At the start of our third night, we stopped for *"exactement cinq minutes"* to eat our cracker snacks and some grapsies. I gave mine to Sunshine because he was used to gladiator rations and needed more food than the rest of us. He reached out to take my offerings, and the ground opened up and swallowed him.

He came up out of the muddy water of the sinkhole gagging and flailing. We started hauling him out - God he was heavy! - and all the while we were pulling, the sides of the sinkhole kept collapsing, making the hole bigger and bigger. We backed up and up and up until we were stopped by a huge boulder. Sunshine pulled himself onto it, his muscles bulging and strained, his face contorted. Anybody else would have been washed away.

As soon as we had him on solid ground, we all ran like hell. I turned once and saw the boulder falling into the still-expanding sinkhole. Trees followed. Hundreds of the three-times-replanted trees of the Chairman's forest just crumpled and sank. *Once to destroying...*

Almost losing Sunshine really scared me. I mean, when the ground is opening up underneath you, and you can't know whether the hole is going to close or continue growing until it swallows you and your friends and everything you want out of life, well, that really makes you think about the power of dumb luck and other serious things.

Following Grandma's example, I tried to lighten the mood by teaching the guys "The Rains of April."

A whole tribe of turtles showed up to listen.

They lifted their long necks out from under their shells and swayed their heads to the music. My cousin Athena, who has studied zoology, once told me that turtles live a long long time, so I guess they must have been old enough to recognize that ancient song.

"*Notre premiere!*" Willy announced. "*L'audience nos adore!* Perhaps we shall to calling ourselves 'Le Tall Band.' What do you thinking of that? *Allons y tous!*"

Le Tall Band marched on, followed by a parade of its turtle fans. As we came to the end of the Chairman's forest, they one by one waggled their heads "goodbye" and dropped out and went home.

Only one stayed. She was the most loyal turtle. Willy suggested we call her Cordelia.

She followed us all the way to the gateway to Eddie's camp. It looked like she was planning to follow us inside.

I concluded that she must be one of Jedda's spies.

I screamed "Run! Go go go run!"

I picked up a heavy rock and dropped it on Cordelia, ready to toss the pieces of her back into the forest.

Splat.

No explosion.

Just splat.

Oh God.

IN EDDIE'S CAMP

Grandpa was living halfway up a mountain with a whole big bunch of other people. Their weather station hid itself among the dense thickets, eyes peeking out like the antennae of bugs. We made our homes in caves that had sheltered guerilla fighters during the food wars. We got our heat from solar collectors and smokeless fires made from logs of compressed algae, the same kind of logs that had burned up Great Uncle Clyde's body.

It was like a little town. Grandpa was sort of the CEO. Except he didn't own 85% of anything. If he needed to say something important to someone, he just took them aside and spoke to them privately.

Of course we had rules. You were never allowed to kill an animal except in self-defense and never ever a pregnant animal or a baby animal, not even if it was a wildcat or a buzzard, because a baby was a sign of a family and the return, even in some tiny way, of the old nature. (For this reason, the members of Le Tall Band took a solemn vow not to tell how I had brutally murdered poor Cordelia.)

You had to absolutely do your job in Eddie's camp. If you didn't, you got kicked out, and what would you do then? I mean, halfway up a mountain in the middle of nobody knew where? So everybody worked. I tended the stunted, gnarly apple trees and the berry bushes, collected certain spicy leaves for tea and helped Farah take care of the swallows.

We had ginormous herds of swallows. They nested in the trees and blacked out the camp at night. We got used to the noise they made. (Although I personally never got used to the poop.) If we found one dead, we laid it down in one of the short corn patches for the crows to come and eat. If the snakes got there first, the crows would eat them too. Farah said the swallows left the camp once a year to return to a certain southern spot where they would socialize and select mates and get pregnant. Then they would find us again, ready to resume their jobs as delivery birds.

The short corn grew in little patches here and there; no big fields that might catch the attention of overflying suncopters. Grandpa told me that the seed for it had been brought to the camp by an old Mexican lady, now dead. Eleven stolen kernels of Corporation seed, programmed not to germinate unless planted on Corporation land according to Corporation protocols. The old lady buried each kernel in a terra cotta bead and wore them scattered among 87 other identical beads in her necklace. In case the beads were damaged, she had some extra kernels in her ears behind her hearing aids.

She could have been disappeared for stealing those seeds.

She planted her kernels in a hill of sand and dirt and assorted poop mixed with rotting tea leaves. Added a swallow feather mulch. Said prayers. Everybody thought she was nuts. But then two of the seeds busted out of their chemical destiny and grew into stumpy little corn plants, which produced seeds that produced another generation of little corn plant babies and *pow!* an actual non-Corporate crop was on its way. They named the corn "Abuela." Now we had enough to make some flat bread.

Outgoing communication was forbidden in Eddie Bright's camp. You could receive messages, see the faces, hear the voices, *but you could not answer.* An iron clad rule, meant to keep our location secret from Jedda's spies.

If Grandpa thought we had been found, he would move us, instantly. You never in your life saw a whole big bunch of people melt away so fast.

"Is it not puzzling, *mes enfants,*" said Willy on one occasion when we were melting away, "that these officials in St. Paul with their lenses and their sunflights cannot to capturing a bunch of defenseless trouble makers on a mountain?"

"Maybe they don't want to capture us," I said. "Maybe they just want to keep an eye on us and know what we are doing."

"Ah," said Willy, smiling at me.

Sunshine, Paco and I began playing music together on a regular basis. Willy Sachertorte became our teacher.

He arranged our music and gave us lessons. We got used to his weird Franglaisish talk and his fancy metaphors. He made us practice just as we would have done if we had gone to Bloomington, hours and hours every day. Paco's fingers seemed to grow extra joints. Sunshine acquired new kinds of drums that had to be played with sticks and padded mallets. I began learning French. I sang scales and more scales and gained my octave.

Willy had a thing about enunciation. My first teacher, Mrs. Lightfinger, focused on breath, the diaphragm, and developing the muscles that supported the lungs. But Willy insisted that an equally important engine of the voice was the mouth - the teeth, the tongue, the resonant palates - and the wide open throat, and these were controlled by the big muscle of the brain.

"Willy say: '*Chaque letter de chaque mot* to delivering feeling. *Attend, cherie.* Willy want you to looking this word. *Pillow.* Strong *p* to sending message of hard, maybe even angry." He pursed his lips. Scrunched his face. "Strong *ow* to sending message of *douceur.*" He rolled his eyes upward, rounded his mouth. "Oh ohhhh...ohhhh sooooh sweet! *Et maintenant*...strong *lls* to making peoples to smiling.

"Willy say: 'Each letter to coloring the word, and the word is to being the message and the melody is to being its lover that hides it away from the danger of to being forgotten, in a special corner of the brain where it lives, *aux bras de la melodie,* forever.'"

Farah the sparrow herder taught us a song called "Marble Banks." Grandpa didn't want us to sing that because, he said, its lyrics attacked the whole concept of profit on which our continental government was based, and if our rendition ever leaked onto The Beam, Horatio Jedda might stop trying to convince us to return with his nice, hope-laden messages and just send an army of ordermen to shut us down.

So then Farah taught us "Four Generals." Grandpa took her aside and spoke to her privately. She promised not to teach us any more revolutionary tunes, but of course she did.

We practiced. Willy made us new arrangements. We took lessons and practiced. We learned "My Old Mule Sal" and "At the Clear Fountain" in French, which Willy arranged so it could be sung right along with "The Rains of April." We changed our line-up all the time.

Just as Grandma had promised, it was music school.

What I had been dreaming of for years.

Heaven.

At night we turned on the lady bug and sang our songs for the whole camp. Eddie's people loved to hear "Buffalo Girls" and most particularly "Miss Betsy from Pike", a funny old singalong song from the days of plenty. But I swear we had no idea that somebody was sending our music to The Beam -- until one night Sergei the carpenter heard us right in the middle of the boat construction show. Suddenly instead of the hearty shipwright talking, it was us singing "Don't Cry Suzanna" out of his face. After a few minutes, his voice came back and our song disappeared. Another time, Sigmund, our camp doctor, caught a North African rock band on the surgery show. Hypnotic drums and twangling ouds, he said. Men singing in unison and a lady soloist with a trill like a quavering reed.

Concerts came to one or another of us, in punchy little snatches, you could never know when or on which Incoming. A salsa band from the Brazilian interior. Gospel singers from Denmark. Opera from Italy.

Grandpa's resident tech, Fred, told us that the music break-ins originated in Anatolia. Some talented hacker there was picking up performances around the world and sending them out wherever they could be made to land. The Chinese Imperial Radiobeam and the Caliphate Network were being hit as well. People called the hacker "Pan Neutrino" because he was magic: country-less and body-less, hidden in a new kind of soundray that shimmied through the earth's very core and couldn't be tracked. Pan Neutrino.

Our cook, Shulamit, who had Latino relatives on her father's side, taught us how to dance.

I danced with everybody. I danced and danced and sang and sang in Grandpa Eddie's camp.

Once long ago there had been a quarry up on our mountain. People dug stone out of the ground with huge machines. They often set off explosions to loosen the stone, which was of a sort that broke straight and square along fault lines within itself. They used the stone for paving and building blocks and tomb markers back in the days when it was actually safe and legal to bury dead people individually in real wooden coffins in the ground.

The hole from which they extracted the stone had filled up with water over the centuries. Since the hole had been dug from solid rock, no dirt in there, no plants, the water was crystal clear and freezing cold. By midday the sun had warmed the top few feet enough for me to swim across and back a couple of times.

Heedful of Grandma's advice, I swam for the sake of maintenance. I swam to keep the muscles that supported my lungs powerful and pliable, so as not to neglect the lessons Mrs. Lightfoot had taught me. I got better and better at swimming. I could swim longer and longer every day. Not fast, just long. Breathe. Stroke. Breathe. Stroke. Breathe.

On the edge of the lake, I sat on a warm rock, and I swear, the earth around me seemed to be just like what Grandma described from when she was a girl. Clean water, friendly sun, real birds singing. It was such a perfect moment that I almost didn't look at my Incoming when it called.

My attitude toward the familiar buzz had changed. It felt like a disturbance. Since I was forbidden to answer it, I wasn't interested in it any more. Then I saw that it was Nikolai. He kept a big shaggy dog in front of himself. But I could see his black eyes behind the fur. An antiseptic smell wafted off him into my fresh outdoorsy day. I realized he was in a hospital! How could I not answer him?

"Are you hiding behind that dog?"

"Yes. I've been scratched up. My dog looks better than I do."

"Scratched up? Why do I think that sounds like a load of baloney?"

"Because you are a clever person. Never mind. I will be fine in time. Where are you?"

"I can't actually say. But my life is wonderful now. I've been swimming in a beautiful lake. I have a singing lesson in five minutes."

"Ah, you have found a teacher."

"A great teacher. And I have a band. Three out of the four of us are six feet or over, so we are called Le Tall Band. We have lots of new songs. Every night we sing for the people here. Pan Neutrino... have you heard of him?"

"Everyone has heard of him."

"He's been putting us on The Beam. One time we actually heard ourselves, and these other singers too, Nikolai, wonderful musicians. God, I wish you were really here with us. What you said to me, in St. Paul, it made me feel so much better. It made me strong again."

"Sing me one of your new songs, Lizzie."

"What time is it where you are? Is it night? Sunshiney day?"

"It is twilight."

It took me a couple of minutes. But then the right thing came to me.

Though the heart be weary,
Sad the day and long,
Still to us at twilight
Comes love's old song,
Comes love's old sweet song.

Nikolai lifted himself from behind the dog. He had five long vertical scars on one cheek, like a musical staff upended. His left hand had only three fingers.

In front of everybody, Grandpa called me an idiot. An inconsiderate, thoughtless, self-involved idiot. I had given away our location to Jedda's agents in order to sing a song to a dog, and now the whole camp had to move.

Grandpa really knows how to make you feel bad.

I guess Mom learned it from him.

Could I have defended myself? I guess so. I could have said *Oh come on, Grandpa, get real. I didn't give anything away. One of those sparrows has got to be a spy, just like Shankar, and the Corporation probably knows exactly where we are and what we are doing every minute.* But wouldn't that have shown how little I respected him, undermined his authority, hurt his feelings? I mean he was my Grandpa. He was old. He came from the time when hiding from the authorities was possible. Sometimes you just have to keep your mouth shut and give your loved ones a break.

So I was in disgrace.

All the while we were melting into the forest under cover of the swallow blanket, nobody would speak to me.

Every shiver of the trees made Farah and Shulamit and the gang think that ordermen were coming to arrest us, that we would be attacked from above, blanketed with aero-poison, or shot selectively by drone bullets that said REBELLION

But then it turned out, of course, that this Horatio Jedda guy never had any intention of sending his ordermen to overrun

Eddie's camp — because he had much bigger things to worry about.

PART THREE

11. EMMY was being blown westward...

*E*MMY was being blown westward, toward Kazakhstan, where the seedlings of the wheat crop would break ground in May. She picked up speed by traveling inside the funnel of a bellowing tornado, the last in a series of 16 that had ransacked the steppes of north central Asia during March and April.

When the storm dissipated and the farmers emerged from their underground shelters to view the newest damage, EMMY hung in the air above them.

She followed along with the farmers as they trudged across their fields. She hovered as they reassembled their printed rice board houses. Invisible. Waiting.

It gently rained. The nights were cool. The farmers and their families smiled. EMMY smiled for the first time since winter's end. Perfect weather. Soon the new crop was peeking through the soil.

EMMY floated upward on the evening breezes, anticipating that wonderful moment when the seedlings would have grown just a little taller, and she could pounce.

Then the heat wave exploded.

Temperatures soared. The rain withdrew into heaven. The irrigation water, carefully collected during the year's deluges, was popped by rationed droplets into the fields. By June, the grass on the steppes had crinkled and turned to straw and the grazing herds could find nothing to eat.

The land cracked, becoming dust.

The tornadoes came back.

They swirled the dust into the air where it just hung like a curtain across all of creation. Gentle lambs, cloned from one mother, raised in labs, lay asphyxiated on the range, their identical legs sticking up.

The irrigation water had to be reassigned to drinking. The wheat seedlings withered.

Like the farmers and their families, EMMY faced starvation.

Desperate for a way out of the Kazakh oven, EMMY turned east, riding on the winds above the raiders who had begun sneaking across the border to hijack Chinese water tankers and sell the water, gallon by gallon, to the thirsty people.

The Empire's response was swift and bloody.

EMMY floated across maimed Kazakh bodies and settled onto the wings of Chinese military sunflights. They carried her yet further east, right into an even more ferocious heat wave.

Now she really didn't know where to turn.

Neither did the people. The Imperial government urged them to hang on, sent synthetic veggies and boxed drinking water and opened the emergency stores of feed grain, assuring everyone that things would certainly get better in the fall. By a stroke of astonishing foresight, the farmers of the North American west coast had planted much more than usual and were already negotiating to sell their hefty surplus at good prices.

Yes, everything would be better in the fall, promised the government.

But many people were not prepared to wait.

There were tantalizing reports that the Ukrainians to the southwest had rain and a bumper crop in the fields. Maybe they would need some extra hands for the harvest. Maybe they would share.

EMMY found a family that had packed up the kids and the bedding and what was left of the herd and hitched herself to them, riding along in the shaggy coat of their ram.

The ram brought her to Ukraine in November, too late to infect this year's crop.

EMMY floated further south, away from winter's ice, and hid out near Yerevan in Armenia, waiting for spring, when the black earth of the Crimea would offer up next year's delicious wheat.

12. THE EMMY FIGHTERS

In September, selected shareholders judged to be pertinent listeners received a disturbing Incoming message. It was from Horatio Jedda, appearing in person, announcing the advent of a mortal threat to the wheat crop.

The Chairman himself had ordered Horatio to appear, judging that the announcement would be taken more seriously if a real live Corporate executive delivered it. Just as important, as Arliss the weatherman pointed out over apple pie and ice cream at "Rose'n'Harry's", if the anti-EMMY program failed, Jedda would be the one held accountable.

Horatio's message came and went quickly. Many selectees missed it. They had to rush around begging others who might be pertinent to share what they had heard.

On the Burton farm, Furlong caught the message in the midst of harvesting. (Petunia and Odin had not been selected, nor had the two field hands.) Stevie Foster suspended operations in his St. Paul lab when he heard Jedda's rasping voice. Athena briefly freed herself from her lover's embrace to pay close attention. (The lover had not been selected.)

Out on the desert in a stinging wind, Itamar missed the message.

Felicity simply ignored it and continued reading the cache of ancient letters, called The Chilean File, which she had discovered on a collecting trip to the southern wilderness.

No one in Eddie Bright's rebel encampment received the message.

Twenty minutes later, everybody in North America received it, whether they qualified as pertinent listeners or not.

Somehow Pan Neutrino had smashed the iron seals of individuated reception. All the isolated little screens pulsed simultaneously with Horatio's nondescript voice and face. In an instant, the mass audience – outlawed for decades – had come back.

If coffee itself had been restored to the earth, there could not have been a more mind-blowing resurrection.

Eddie yelled for everyone to stop what they were doing and pay attention. Shulamit the cook protested. She insisted that Jedda's announcement had nothing to do with them because they hadn't tasted anything made with wheat since their arrival in the mountains. Many of Eddie's followers agreed and went back to doing what they had been doing.

Eddie did not take anybody aside this time. He just roared. "Are you alone on this planet?! If someone else starves, do you think that has nothing to do with you?! Forget the decency piece. I am ready to believe that living under the government of a profit-driven corporation has erased all human sympathy from your hearts. But you can bet that when the wheat eaters start seeing their kids go hungry, they will show up at our door and they'll be ready to do anything, *anything!* to put bread on the table again."

He singled out his granddaughter, Lizzie, because he was already so mad at her. "Your father, Lizzie...did you think he died because unfeeling crazies attacked NewLA for no reason? He died because some hungry girl's father wanted her to have your dinner."

So Eddie's people, like millions of other North American shareholders, settled down to hear what Horatio Jedda had to say.

"We are in great danger," he said. "A new disease has been discovered that can destroy an entire wheat harvest in a matter of weeks. She is called EMMY. She is a modern race of an ancient plague known as stem rust. Every authorized wheat variety in the world is vulnerable."

The specter of EMMY devouring wheat plants poured off every Incoming, surrounding the horrified viewers.

"If we don't defeat EMMY quickly, she could return us to the days of famine. Corporate scientists are working around the clock to invent a medicine called EMMY-B-GONE that will protect the harvest. We are meeting with all branches of the Agroclans Society to access every possible input from farmers on the ground. The Agrotech Division will keep everyone informed as events develop." He paused. Rubbed his eyes. "I'm really sorry to have to be the bearer of such disturbing news. Thank you for your attention."

In Eddie's camp, a few people commented that Jedda actually seemed like a nice guy. One might even be tempted to trust him.

"Try not to be so dumb and gullible, folks," Eddie Bright snapped. "Horatio Jedda is a Corporation creature. He doesn't speak unless he lies."

HORATIO

He was indeed lying.

Horatio held it as an article of faith not to announce the existence of a problem until he had the solution in hand.

This precept he had learned from his great grandmother, a gynecologist. She had once told him that menopause was never considered an actual disease for which you needed to buy preventive medicine, until someone had already discovered how to extract estrogen from a Mexican yam.

Corporate scientists were not "working around the clock" to invent EMMY-B-GONE, as Horatio had said. They had already developed the poison. It had already been manufactured and stored in secret warehouses all over North America when he made his announcement.

As he had foreseen, the Chemical Division had needed only a few weeks to develop the anti-EMMY fungicide. The Bioengineering Group had taken another three weeks to condense the fungicide into a pellet. Each pellet had a solar-powered distribution mechanism and eight sides. Each side could keep 100 acres EMMY-free for at least six weeks. A normal growing season would require only one set of replacements.

The cost to North American farmers would be high, the cost to foreigners much higher.

Horatio's "short way" plan had been speeding along, right on schedule.

Then the Chairman himself nearly derailed it.

He allowed that bunch of nit-picking fops in the Packaging Division to fritter away *months* assembling a box design that each member of the Board could approve.

This delay brought Horatio's plan right up to the brink of the spring sowing. Had EMMY appeared in north central Asia this year, as expected, the Manufacturing Division would have had no product to ship just when desperate farmers were demanding an antidote. In the value system of the Corporation, nothing could destroy a man's reputation faster than missing out on a season of global monopoly. Horatio's "short way" scenario would have been a bust, his ambitions to succeed the Chairman destroyed.

"The Chairman did this deliberately," Esmerelda Wolf said. "To hurt you."

"Hanging around with spies has made you excessively suspicious."

"That doesn't mean I'm wrong. He's enraged that you appeared before a mass audience."

"He put me there."

"And now regrets it."

"I can't be held responsible for the shenanigans of a Turkish hacker."

"You can be," said the iron-faced woman. "You are being."

Horatio knew she was right. By sending out the EMMY message to all and sundry, the damn Turk had made Horatio into a bit of a celebrity. The Chairman, long accustomed to using Horatio's ideas for his own advancement, now had reason to believe that his HR expert might be using them to advance himself.

Horatio had counted on the Chairman's support. Instead he would have to contend with his jealousy.

Luckily, EMMY herself had torpedoed the Chairman's attempt to discredit Horatio, simply by disappearing.

"EMMY's gone into hiding from the East Asian heat wave," Stevie Foster reported. "She's overwintering somewhere, waiting for next year. Next year is gonna be hell."

That was fine with Horatio.

Next year, just when the wheat seedlings were popping out of the ground, and EMMY was ready to infect them, he would order EMMY-B-GONE, in its new, colorful, sweet-smelling boxes, released from the secret warehouses *as though it had just been discovered.* And desperate farmers everywhere would eagerly buy it to protect their crop.

"The short way" safety net had been finessed. And there was still plenty of time for The Grain Guardians to complete the far preferable "long way" – the development of wheat seed genetically modified to resist EMMY.

PEPPER

To know what his competitors were planning, Horatio sent his own beloved black spaniel, Pepper, to China. There, posing as an orphan stray, Pepper ingratiated himself with the children of Dr. Chow Sam, Stevie Foster's opposite number and arguably the world's greatest wheat breeder.

Pepper loved being a spy. He loved Horatio. He felt really proud to be such a well-connected member of the elite intelligence organization, SPICE, which served as North America's most potent instrument of industrial espionage.

SPICE recruited shareholders who demonstrated exceptional powers to communicate non-verbally. Horatio called them "the strong of thought." Often, they had been deaf and/or blind as children or as a result of some unhappy event in peace or war, and subsequently cured.

Esmerelda Wolf was their leader.

Each SPICE agent received a brand new blank SPICEbot, built like a baby animal, to program and train. The agent-SPICEbot teams were matched, human for machine, neuron for circuit, and shared a unique common language. Sometimes the bot had a secret SPICE name as well as a cover name. (The little red bird Shankar, murdered by Eddie Bright, had been christened originally "Cumin" by his agent-partner, Foxie's cook.)

No matter how distant from the agent, the SPICEbot could always hear the agent's thoughts and do the agent's bidding.

For example, every week Esmerelda Wolf sent a thought directive to her SPICEbot, Thyme, a huge American bald eagle, to drop a sacrificial rat into the New Dead Sea as a test.

Was the poison in the water abating? Could anything survive in that awful stew? Could anything sink in it?

Thyme reported back to Esmerelda telepathically.

The results of the rat-drops remained in her head.

If everything went well, at the close of a two-year term of service, the agents were retired with handsome settlements, and their beloved creatures reprogrammed for less dangerous jobs.

If something bad happened to the SPICEbot or the agent — capture, torture, accident, death -- the bot exploded, and the neurological connections to it in the agent's brain short-circuited and died.

Horatio had dutifully explained this death pact to Pepper, holding the little dog in his arms and weeping at the thought of such a parting. No tears came out, of course. But Pepper was in Horatio's soul, and he knew his boss was crying and would be broken hearted if anything bad happened to him.

Pepper played with Dr. Chow's kids and befriended his assistants. He slept in a soft bed in the corner of Chow's lab where the busy Incomings buzzed.

In short order he was transmitting all of Chow's research to Horatio Jedda.

ITAMAR

Itamar Mugombo and his husband, Stan, had once lived on a farm in Maine. They had vegetables and geese, perennials and nut trees. They led mushroom-hunting classes. Every week during the harvest season, they hosted a dinner for the entire community. Everybody cooked, everybody served, everybody ate.

When the ocean overran the coast and hungry refugees arrived, Itamar and Stan tried to keep their dinners going even though they had more mouths to feed from the same old harvest. Then raiders invaded from the north, burning and looting, devouring everything, killing Stan.

Clyde Bright sent a message of condolence. It contained an invitation: *If you ever feel the need of a safe place to work, come to us.*

In due course, Itamar wrenched himself away from his home and his memories, and joined The Grain Guardians.

He took up an ancient religion that admonished him to meditate, radiate beneficence and wear diaphanous clothing. He had a habit of peering directly into your eyes when he spoke to you, as though he were searching behind your words, trying to read your true mind. Esmeralda Wolf, who gave everybody the creeps, said Mugombo gave her the creeps.

Horatio concurred. However, Mugombo was a great scientist. From microbial dust, he re-created orchards. In his greenhouses at The Sun Project on the Mohave Spread, he grew date palms and olive trees and strawberries, thought to be lost forever. He herded scorpions for their venom, which proved invaluable as a basis for certain anti-inflammatory medicines. It was rumored that he even raised flowers.

Nobody knew about Itamar's kids.

Most of the kids were orphaned pirates, exactly as in the ancient operetta, which Itamar's grandmother had taken him to see as a child. But instead of being funny, they were ferocious and hate-filled, bent on revenge for drowned places. Sri Lanka.

Costa Rica. Vancouver. Their mothers had been off shore whores who worked on floating brothels, long, flat vessels, garlanded with red lights and casting music like a net across the sea. Their fathers had been members of the deadly Baha raiders.

The pirates in their agile boats hid among the inlets and channels that 150 years of regular tsunamis had torn into the coast. They assaulted the algae trawlers mining the red tides of the dead zones. They boarded research ships that were pouring lab-raised baby fish into the ocean and trying to start up a semblance of sea life once again, and held the scientists on board for fat ransoms. They captured the pleasure vessels of wealthy tech smugglers who dared to compete with the established powers. Such outlaws would willingly make a good deal. If they would not, one could always turn them over to the authorities for a price.

Every order-keeping force on earth was hunting the pirates. The kids born into this life had no hope of an education or a moment's peace -- until Itamar took them in.

He hid them near the scorpion tanks where he felt sure no one would go searching, and fed them by padding his grocery accounts. Of course, some returned to the sea to become feared raiders along the Pacific coast. However, others gave up the pirate life and came to work for The Sun Project.

They learned to maintain the solar collectors that blanketed New Mexico, Arizona and Eastern California now that those places had become so hot that neither man nor beast could live there anymore. Or they became apprentices in the desert greenhouse system.

Itamar took the kids along on his archeobotany expeditions and taught them how to read the old maps, so they could see that once not so long ago, this wasteland was bursting with wells of fresh, clean water, with kale and cattle, plump juicy melons and nimble horses.

"We are looking for wheat," he told the kids on the search team near the ruins of Tucson. "Ancient wheat plants which may have left a trace of their DNA in these desert sands. Pan and sift, children. Pan and sift, just as though you were mining for gold. Sometimes an ancient variety will contain genes for immunity that have long been thought extinct. And if we are patient and thorough, we may perhaps resurrect such a rare grain and bring it to maturity and send it to Dr. Foster in St. Paul so he can save our people from EMMY."

FELICITY AND ATHENA

The Antarctic Germplasm Bank of the North American Corporation contained almost all the material for growing all the plants that still could grow or had once grown on planet earth.

Billions of seeds were stored there, dried and frozen, and so were chunks of the plants that didn't grow from seed, in vaults deep down under the ice. If something happened to the farms — and something was always happening to the farms -- the bank was the place to go for new seed to start over.

Dozens of such banks had existed in previous centuries. The Chinese national collection had contained millions of accessions for every variety of soy, rice, wheat, bamboo. Felicity Bjornsdottir had done her postdoctoral work there, a slender, golden-haired girl setting hearts on fire in the archives.

She went home to North America for the funeral of her father and all his shipmates, killed in the Battle of Fundy, the last great naval engagement of the food wars. While she was away, the big dam broke back in China. All the seeds and all her friends were swept away.

The many Indian germplasm banks were raided and their contents devoured during the famine. The Russian collections, including everything Dr. Nikolai Vavilov had acquired in his 20th century travels around the world, were wiped out in the flash fires that obliterated St. Petersburg and its outlying suburbs. The archipelago collections in England and Japan disappeared beneath the seas. In Mexico, a bank specializing in wheat and corn ended up buried under miles of ash and lava when the volcano blew.

The massive earthquakes which had reconfigured Colorado took out the old American collection.

Felicity told her students that the desert seed banks – the big one in Syria, the littler ones in Egypt and Israel – were attacked during the famine by "criminal dumbos."

"They heard *bank* and thought *money,*" she said. "When all they found was seeds, they got mad and tossed everything on the ground and mushed it around into a useless jumble. Barley, plum trees, ro...ro...roses." She showed the young people pictures of the gorgeous blossoms. "No babies. No future. Gone from this world forevforevevev...."

The only large comprehensive germplasm bank remaining was the facility in Antarctica. And thanks to Horatio Jedda, it belonged to the Corporation, which had used the seeds as the genetic basis for synthetic foods that saved North America's shareholders from starvation. If some misfortune should befall the big bank, copies of its accessions could be found in thousands of small secret places all around North America and its southern plantations, an emergency back-up system, guarded by ever-changing codes and implacable devices programmed to kill.

Workers in the germplasm bank were supposed to serve under the ice for a maximum of six months at one tour of duty. When EMMY appeared, many tours were extended indefinitely, among them that of Lizzie's cousin, Athena Burton.

For more than a year now, she had been working long days in the stem rust collections and the agrohistory files, looking for directions to some set of genes, somewhere in the vast extended family of *triticum,* which might provide 22nd century wheat with immunity to the plague.

Athena was dispatched down to the lowest vaults, where the rescued records of human agriculture were stored. Felicity had named this place "Alexandria."

At her boss's insistence, Athena summoned up from Alexandria the field books of ancient explorers. "Maybe they came across a variety that didn't get stem rust," Felicity explained. "Maybe some local variety somewhere…" The reports of such famous plant hunters as Vavilov, Mark Carleton and Harry and Jack Harlan had long ago been stored in virtual data banks. But thousands of others, from less famous collectors, remained under preservative seals in their original paper form.

The field books rose up out of the archives on jets of wind. Stacks of pages of real paper, crumbling, filled with faded, scrawny notes in *handwriting*, a skill almost completely disappeared, in Polish and Norwegian, Spanish and Japanese. Endless ruminations on blooming time, awn length and bygone pollinators now sat on Athena's desk like her own personal mountains, demanding that she climb.

It was a nightmare.

Felicity summoned experts on cursive script. Everything was translated. Nothing helped.

Athena dreamed of her warm California home. She ached and sighed with longing. Her newest lover kissed her and hugged her and tried to make her feel better, but his tenderness was no match for EMMY.

Felicity had lately become obsessed with the papers of an ancient Chilean seed banker. He had made a trip to Tibet in the late twentieth century to collect grains. He had covered the same terrain that Vavilov had covered seventy years earlier.

The Russian botanist had mentioned collecting a kind of wheat in Tibet that was armed with a purplish pigment to protect it while living so close to the sun. The Chilean plant collector reported having seen it as well.

This wheat reportedly never got sick. It was called Lucky Boy. Like so many other plants, it had disappeared.

All of Vavilov's samples, and all of their copies, were gone.

Felicity hoped that the Chilean collector might have brought back his own samples of Lucky Boy and stashed them someplace — a little freezer, a cellar, a dry box — that might have survived the catastrophes and the wars.

But no. His papers reported that he had returned home with nothing. Not one seed of any plant.

Why? Felicity wondered. Why go all the way to Tibet to hunt for plants and see something so important and return with no sample?

She and Athena were hiking across the glacier for their daily outdoor conference, snow shoes gliding. It wasn't easy to discuss plant genetic diversity under these circumstances, but Felicity insisted that some conversations simply had to be held in private.

Being 20 years old, and a North American shareholder, Athena had never experienced privacy. It meant nothing to her. In public, in private, wherever, she was determined to make her beloved teacher face the truth.

"We're getting nowhere, Professor."

"The Chilean File has the ans...ans..."

"I've read The Chilean File many times. Really, there's nothing useful in it. Just a bunch of old personal letters."

"He went to Tibet. He says that he came across the wheat that Vavilov called Lucky B...B...B... the wheat that doesn't get sssss....."

"But he didn't *come home* with Lucky Boy, Professor. And it was more than 150 years ago. And just because the wheat he talks about didn't get stem rust *then* doesn't mean that it wouldn't get EMMY *now*, even if we could find it, which we can't."

"Maybe the Ch...Ch..."

"If the Chinese had it, and it contained genes that conferred resistance to EMMY, the Chinese would be marketing resistant wheat right this minute and desperate farmers everywhere would be buying it. They haven't got it, Professor. Because it doesn't exist. The samples that Vavilov collected burned up in the Russian fires. All the copies that may have been made are apparently gone. So now, like millions of other varieties, it is extinct and lost to us. Lucky Boy has become a myth, Professor. It is a character in a story in a museum. We cannot go on believing in it. The truth is, stem rust has simply found a way to outlive the genes that might once have prevented it." Athena channeled her mother,

Petunia. "I say we contact Dr. Foster in St. Paul and tell him we've struck out and we've got to give up and he should just go ahead and poison EMMY."

Felicity had stopped moving. Her eyes seemed to be gazing inward. Athena could see that she was getting one of her big ideas.

"Professor Bjornsdottir? Did you hear what I said?"

The fat professor's attention had clearly shifted. She smiled to herself and chewed on the end of her braid.

"Professor Bjornsdottir, please, come back, listen to me. Please."

"Didn't Dr. Jedda once write a paper about China?"

"Yes," Athena said. "His dissertation. About Chinese agricultural policy in the late 20th century. But we were talking about EMMY, Professor."

"Let's find that paper."

"You must see that we are on the verge of a real crisis here. Some of our people feel like they're chasing sunspots. Some of us...them...are beginning to fall apart."

"It's probably down in Alexandria. Let's go back right now and dig it out."

Felicity swerved, snow-shoeing resolutely back toward the germplasm bank. The stuttering had stopped, a sign of single-minded focus on whatever new thing had seized her imagination. Athena knew there would be no retrieving her.

Frustrated that her big appeal had fallen so flat, the young assistant heaved a disappointed sigh. "I guess we can talk again tomorrow."

"Talk?"

"About EMMY, Professor."

"And who is she?"

It was hopeless, Athena thought. Not only were they searching for lost germplasm in the black hole of botanical history, their leader was a wacko genius who had been hospitalized for clinical depression and so energetically medicated that now she changed the subject in the middle of a sentence and couldn't remember what she had been saying ten seconds before.

Felicity stopped abruptly, picked up some snow and licked it.

"You know there was a time, long long ago," she said, "when all this snow around us was owned by no one. It belonged to itself and just gave itself away to anybody who wanted a taste. Dr. Bright used to say that much of the old nature was like that, like a big yummy ice cream cone.

"Did you ever have an ice cream cone, um…um…"

"Athena," Athena said.

STEVIE

Stevie enlisted dozens of his former students, many of them now professors and Corporate consultants, on a top priority, maximum security basis to work at his lab in St. Paul. Naturally they brought their own robots. Stevie's robot corps taught the newcomers everything they needed to know about the task at hand.

They laid out EMMY's genetic map, side by side with the genetic maps of the authorized wheats, then trolled the twin highways, looking for the points of crossing. If they could find the EMMY genes that carried the infection, they could know what they needed to cripple. Then they might be able to discover an enzyme or a protein or some other biochemical interference that would change the infecting gene's function or prevent it from maturing.

But tracking the interactions of grain and disease had grown more and more complicated as more and more traits had been added to help wheat survive in the wild new conditions brought on by climate change. Stevie himself had programmed hundreds of traits into Galveston and Abilene and Waco. Traits to make the wheat withstand sub-zero cold immediately followed by blazing heat, to make it taste bad to birds and good to goats, to keep it growing in limited daylight, in endless daylight, to make it tolerate flooding by sea water and watering by sewage, traits to restore the vitamins and other nutrients that had been lost by the insertion of traits to protect the wheat against chemical poisons in the soil. Somewhere, among the millions of genetic snips and splices that made all the traits possible, there were pathways where EMMY entered, with no trait to stop her. But where?

"Come on, gang," Stevie urged. "Gotta look harder. Gotta find the soft spots."

The scientists worked 14-hour days and fell bleary-eyed into their beds. The robots worked 24-hour days and paused only for deprogramming in the morning.

Even with the tireless staff, the lightning fast computational machinery, there was just too much work. They needed help.

Stevie pleaded to Horatio. "We've need the best minds in the world, not just the best minds in North America. We need Chow Sam and his people in Beijing. For God's sake, unlock my Outgoing so I can reach him at his lab."

"Professor Chow no longer has a lab. He has been detained by the authorities."

"What?! Why?!"

"Because he was caught trying to get in touch with you."

Stevie slammed his fist on the lab table so hard that the little robots jumped and toppled and had to retrace all their calculations to get back on track. "Our situation is too damn serious for this kinda political bullshit!" he cried.

Horatio's vague features seemed now to disappear completely into a blank mask of scorn.

"This kind of political bullshit, as you put it, is the lifeblood of our continent, Professor. We have noted all your attempts to bypass your Outgoing and share top secret information with our competitors, acts that could prevent the people of North America from enjoying a profitable monopoly in international sales of EMMY-resistant seed. In my world they call that treason."

The word landed as accurately as the drone bullet which might at any time deliver it. Stevie sagged into a chair. Sweat pooled in his eyebrows. His nose was running. Jedda kept talking.

"However, unlike Dr. Chow, you are still here at your desk and not in a cell. I beg you to believe that my forbearance can end at any time. Try not to speed the arrival of that moment. Now then. If you will check your Incoming, you will see that while you have been whining, we have been providing you with all of Dr. Chow's research, decoded and ready for use. So please. Just do your job and get us a wheat seed that can stand up to EMMY."

Stevie began to laugh.

They knew everything.

They knew everything, and he belonged to them, and there was no way out.

His Incoming buzzed, announcing a call from China.

He thought miserably that it was probably Chow Sam's wife, calling to say he had been arrested. Possibly worse. Sam.

After a moment of hesitation while the call was scanned and approved for relay, it rang through. A sweet-faced Chinese woman with short blonde hair and green eyes sat down at Stevie's lab table.

"Hello, Dr. Foster. I am Dr. Fong Billy Joe of Blessed Mother Heavenly Rest hospital in Zhigen. I am sorry to report that your assistant has been mauled by a bear. He will have to remain here in hospital for several days while his flesh is being regenerated. Will your lab accept the cost for this treatment?"

13. THE HIMALAYAN KID

Nikolai's journey to his home had begun auspiciously during a window of wonderful weather on the Tibetan plateau.

A Chinese hovervan flew him low across the green meadow. The aged driver spoke fondly of the days before this exotic greenness. The flat plains of his boyhood had been brown, he said, dusted with sturdy brown forage, and green only on the shores of the rivers that swirled through the plateau like thin silver snakes. That silver thinness had vanished as well. Now the rivers rumbled, wild and wide, fed by melting ice that had never melted before. Now the mountains on the horizon glittered with feeder streams that rushed downward toward the plains. The driver remembered them covered, all year round, with ice and snow, immutable, home to philosophies of immortality. These days it was as warm as India here. Temperatures this high had not touched the Himalayas since the dawn of human history.

Nikolai knew all this was true, but he didn't care. The old man's past was way past. And Nikolai was home.

Only nine years before, he had been a boy in this place. It seemed a hundred lifetimes ago.

The driver said that Nikolai's valley, which had been buried in the great mudslide, lay at the other end of the hoverroad pass that crossed through the mountains.

The driver let him out, wished him well and swooshed off into the morning mist.

One had to marvel at the genius of the Chinese hoverroads, hallmark of the nation that had pretty much owned the 21st century. The roads had been built with more than a billion citizens in mind. Now the population of the Empire numbered less than half of that, and people were too poor and chained to their work assignments and tiny home greenhouses to move. The hoverroads lay empty.

Nikolai stood alone on the plateau, facing the mouth of the pass, which cut between two small mountains. They didn't look like real mountains. Maybe they were just old sanitary landfill dumps from the days when people could afford to throw stuff away.

In his pack he carried gear and food for a week's trek. Outside the sunflight port in Zhigen, he had bought a big hunk of delicious cheese made from the milk of real goats. His camera was locked around his wrist on the bracelet right next to his Incoming. His knife was clasped against his left boot.

Stowed in the spine of his pack, he had the ten gallon collapsible box that his beloved mentor, Stevie Foster, had instructed him to bring. "Call it a coffin if you like," the professor had said. "Fill it with earth from the exact spot where your family lived and farmed. Then lock it up tight and wrap it real well. On the outside, put the names of the dead and the names of their animals and their crops. Spray on a protective shield. Don't go buryin' the box up there in the mountains, 'cause a grave has to be visited and you don't know when you'll be able to get back. Keep the box with you, wherever you go.

"Sometimes if you can't find their bones, kid, you've gotta make do with their territory. That's what I did. I keep Texas on my bedside table in a real strong box. It's the next best thing to being there."

The beautiful fall weather made Nikolai think that perhaps the earth was forgiving humanity. The plateau seethed with flowers and flies. As he walked through the pass, he spotted tiny rodents and hopping birds. He carefully avoided stomping on a sleeping lizard. He filled his lungs again and again, drinking the clear thin air, the pale clouds, the blue the blue the azure blue sky as blue as the jewel at her throat...

He chewed a sharp blade of grass. He put on the hat he had never worn in North America, where the sun was so much weaker. Off to his right, he saw the bleached skull of a yak overhung with an arch of tattered banners, fanning prayers into the sky. *Still here. My people are still here.*

He walked for six days, sleeping under the stars, drinking the streams, never meeting a soul, and finally came to the rise in the road that signaled the rim of his valley.

He stood at the rim, and saw... nothing.

The green meadow ended. The hoverroad crashed off the edge, loading docks and passenger stops and repair kiosks scattered for miles in chunks and slabs. The side of the mountain, which had always shadowed the valley, had spilled into it like a bowl of molten lard, a slick, flat blob, and now the mountain was concave and the valley floor lay buried.

Nikolai had known it would be unbearable. That did not make it less unbearable.

To help himself recover from the terrible sight, he closed his eyes and went to sleep. This survival skill - being able to sleep immediately, at will and anywhere, in any position - had been learned during his days on the labor gang. Never had it stood him in such good stead.

When he woke, Nikolai fastened his ropes and rappelled off the edge, lowering himself until the rope ran out. Then he gathered it in a coil, hooked it over his shoulder and continued downward on foot.

The decline into the valley was slippery and precipitous, with no safe way down. The terrain, once littered with rocks and brambles, had become smooth as glass. Nikolai dug slots for his feet and hands, figuring that he would have to come back this way and must leave himself a stairway. Each hole felt like it had to be hacked out of marble.

He felt overjoyed when his pick finally found a soft spot. He dug until he realized he was digging through a partly mummified corpse. Ghastly remainders cascaded out of the hole onto his chest and face.

Nikolai lunged backward in horror, lost his footing and went sliding and rolling down the slick hillside. His pack smashed open. The stowed box, his tools and the remnants of his provisions rocketed away. He landed in the arms of an outcropping tree.

There he lay, gasping, limbs out-flung, facing the sky.

He checked in with his body. Nothing broken.

He was so glad just to be alive that he couldn't make himself move for several minutes. And so the bear found him.

Nikolai looked down at the long black wet snout. This was not one of the country's traditional brown bears who preferred fish and honey to people. This bear was a smaller, voracious omnivore, part black, part whitish yellow, a deadly predator spawned in the melted-together range of polar and grizzly. At first the bear only rocked the little tree, trying to dislodge its human fruit. Then he began tearing at the tree with saber claws.

Nikolai pulled the knife off his boot. The bear reached for his right leg. Nikolai knifed him in the eyes. The bear clawed through his trousers into his shin. Nikolai slashed the tendons of one paw. The bear roared and heaved itself upward, raked Nikolai's face, and tore two fingers from his left hand. Nikolai's knife severed the bear's jugular.

Desperate not to faint and topple into the grasp of the thrashing, mortally wounded animal below, Nikolai hooked the coil of rappelling rope onto a branch of the tree so that he would hang there, and not fall, so that he could faint, and not fall, so that he could give in to the pain and the loss of blood and faint...

Fainting, he heard the report of an ancient rifle and the voice of his dog.

He kept forgetting that the fourth and fifth fingers on his left hand were gone. He grasped the door handle in his hospital room and expected them to be grasping too. But on the handle he saw something that looked like a lobster claw. Below his right hip, he saw what remained of his leg, taped together and currently useless.

Dr. Fong had evened out the stumps of Nikolai's fingers and sent the trimmings to Lhasa for genetic analysis and reproduction. Likewise the cells from his ravaged shin and calf. Nikolai knew he would be repaired eventually. But he feared he might never again be as dexterous as he had always counted on being – and the pain of that was excruciating.

Nikolai's cousin Tencing had saved him. A wiry man, utterly humorless, he tenanted from the Chinese Empire three hundred grazing acres on the Tibetan plateau. He kept a herd of goats and a herd of yaks and three wives (orphaned cousins) and 14 children. He was a licensed hunter, authorized to shoot for their multi-colored pelts the ferocious hybrid bears, and wolves too, that roamed the Himalayan valleys.

Of course Tencing operated within strict government regulations. Killing anything beyond the legal limit could get you hung in the new new China.

Tencing's hunting partner, the fierce mastiff, Oberon, had never forgotten the friend of his youth. He slept next to the wounded leg. When Nikolai moaned from pain, the big dog whimpered with empathy.

Nikolai dreamed through an analgesic haze. She was sitting by a lake in the sun. Beads of water glistened on her arms. Her hair was drying, gold shining on each curl. She was singing to him. He wondered if he would ever see her in the flesh again, if she would ever lie next to him instead of Oberon...

Tencing said that he and Oberon had been out hunting when the mountain collapsed and buried their village. They heard the roar. They took shelter in a cave. They saw the wall of mud descending. They watched the end of everything.

"I believe that I was spared in order to repopulate the earth with our people," Tencing said.

"You were spared by good fortune," Nikolai said.

"Good fortune is a sign from the gods. It is a sign from the gods that I was close by with my gun when the bear was killing you."

"And I will be forever grateful for that," Nikolai said. "But I do not believe it was a sign of anything. Because if it was, then bad luck is also a sign from the gods and our family was buried for some *reason.* I cannot think there was any reason for the death of all those innocent people."

Tencing ignored Nikolai's argument. He believed what he believed, and nothing would convince him otherwise. Doggedly he insisted: "You must stay here and find women with the right genes and have babies and help me make us into a great nation again."

Nikolai marveled that an idea of racial purity, which had taken thousands of years and cost untold millions of lives to be eradicated, could spring back so quickly.

Was it possible that the gods were right? That nothing ever dies?

Stevie Foster took the Medical Group's sedatives. They made him pass out. They obliterated the image of Nikolai being mauled. They made him forget that all his sneaky scientific networking with foreign colleagues had failed, that no genetic barrier to EMMY had yet been found, that a drone bullet called TREASON could wipe him away at any moment.

The persistent buzz of his Incoming insisted him awake. He didn't want to answer. He opened his eyes, saw Felicity, closed his eyes.

"What is it, honey?" he asked, groggy, eyes still closed. "It's nighttime here, did you forget?"

She peeled off the Incoming, bringing the numbing chill of the glacier with her. She stood next to his bed, under a hazed-over, heatless polar sun, wrapped in furs. She looked like an igloo. Steam poured from her mouth. Her nose dripped little icicles. Didn't she realize the censors would see her and would conclude, as Stevie was concluding right now, that she really was crazy and ought to be re-hospitalized right away?

"I found a great file with many personal papers," she said without stuttering. "It concerns an adoption."

"God, Felicity, please, don't..."

"Listen listen. A Chilean scientist who was just like us went to the Himalayas to find a child. But it was impossible to get the child out. Chinese government policy at that time prevented it. Huge mountains of red tape were placed in the way. The authorities didn't want to let the child go because he was such a fine, healthy boy, no diseases. No diseases. None. Finally the scientist gave up and went home without the child. So the child is still there, in the mountains.

"I was thinking we might give it another try, Stevie. This boy really needs to be adopted. He's had so much tragedy in his life. Some of his brothers died in a terrible fire. His sisters were drowned when a dam collapsed. All his other relatives were buried in a mudslide. If he were a lucky boy oh boy oh boy wouldn't we all be happy if we could maybe adopt him..."

"We've talked about this, honey. We can't adopt a child unless we're together in the same place, and they're never gonna let us be together..."

"Where's the...where's the..."

"It's the middle of the night here! I have had a terrible day! I have to go back to sleep! You have to go back inside or your nose is going to freeze off!"

His shouting upset her. Suddenly she could hardly speak.

"But don't you see ummm we need ummm..."

"For God's sakes, Felicity, leave me alone!"

She had begun to weep with frustration.

"Please Stevie please...we need ummm really need......" Stevie started to click her off. "...the the H...H....we really need our Himalayan kid."

Stevie sat up in bed. He turned on the light. Finally, he was wide awake.

He received special permission to contact Nikolai. The Himalayan kid was stretched out on a reclining chair, his mangled leg dangling from spider thin traction pulleys and wrapped in cell application bandages packed with nutrients spurring regrowth of the torn-away tissue. His missing fingers had been replaced but were not yet moving.

"Ah, I am so glad to see you, Professor."

"Same here, kid. Everyone in the lab sends good wishes. How're you feeling?"

"Much better. I have had many comforts. The antique storydisc you sent distracted me from my troubles. So fascinating the way the man and the lion lived together on that raft. And yesterday at twilight, my beautiful friend sang to me."

"Did you retrieve your family's earth?"

"No. I must go back and try again. They say I can go in ten days or so. My cousin and his children will help me dig. They have given me a new coffin to replace the one that flew away."

Nikolai leaned to the side so Stevie could see the replacement coffin. It could hold twice as much territory as the previous one. It was made of a kind of wood long ago used up and disappeared, called ebony, and decorated with inlaid ivory from the tusks of elephants, which no one had seen except in pictures for more than a century, and it was carved all over with scenes that seemed to have been added one after the other, as though by some traveler in a caravan, beholding ever-new wonders on the route. Mongol hunters stalking an antlered buck. Voluptuous Indian ladies beckoning from couches. Floppy-eared Chinese rabbits peeking from behind flowers. And on the lid, galloping Arabian horses, their tails streaming, the borders of their flight demarked with dark red Tibetan beads.

"Well, I'll tell you, that's a helluva lot nicer than the old box," Stevie murmured.

"My cousin bought it for me with the pelt of the bear who tried to kill me."

"You're a lucky man, Nikolai."

"Yessir. So it seems."

"We've arranged for you to be transported back to North America, but the security people say you can't come back here to the lab. You're going to Professor Mugombo's outfit in the

Mohave Spread. You can recuperate there. Get your strength back."

"Yessir."

"He'll be a good mentor for you."

"Yessir."

"You can trust him, kid. You hear me? Whatever job he gives you, that's the right job for you."

"Yessir."

"You just do what he says."

"I will."

"Okay then. I'm done. Gotta get back to work."

"I wanted to say, you look well, Professor Foster. Your current project must suit you."

"Yeah it does. It's good to know what you have to do, finally, after all these years."

14. THE SEDUCTION

When it was discovered that Sunshine Gomez, the gladiator wrestling champion, preferred to play drums with Le Tall Band rather than to enjoy the cushy orderman job he had received as a reward for his athletic victories, steps were taken to punish him.

Speaking for the Corps, Major Sally Kim Lee announced Sunshine's dishonorable discharge, cut off his family's extra food, fuel and water allotments, removed his name from the wrestling records, placed another retiring gladiator into his job and forgot he had ever existed.

Horatio protested that all this retribution verged on overkill.

"We're talking about entertainers here, Sally," he said. "Harmless lightweights whose greatest dream is to become Beam personalities like Arliss and get paid for telling jokes and singing songs. These are marginal people. Silly people. If we take off after them like they're Baha raiders, they will be politicized and could become dangerous. Instead we should co-opt them.

"Look at how the Chairman handled Lizzie Corelli's grandmother back in the day. He took her out of the club where she was singing dangerous songs and made her a well-paid, comfortable jingle singer. That's what we should do with Lizzie and Paco and Willy and Sunshine. Make them *our* troubadours."

Sally laughed at him.

"Please, Dr. Jedda. Let's be a little more clear-headed here, shall we? Foxie Burton Bright has never been 'our troubadour.' She bedded down with whoever could help her. She took the money and the food and the pretty clothes, and the minute she thought she was safe, she went back to being an enemy of the state."

Horatio made a mental note of Sally's intransigence and her particular antipathy toward Foxie as well as her insufferable condescension toward himself. He told Esmerelda to have a Spice agent keep an eye on her.

Mr. and Mrs. El Din admitted to having kidnapped Paco in St. Paul with the help of privately hired gladiators. When they first got him home, he seemed resigned to farming and behaved sweet and peaceful. Then one night, he bolted.

They admitted to having hidden their own privately purchased security cameras in his violin case. These recorded Paco accepting a lift with someone who landed next to him in a custom-built hoverride that could be steered by the driver's own personal hand.

Thus far the driver could not be identified. Some highly advanced anti-spying fog on the windows had made it impossible to see his face. Only his hands and the cuffs of his blue sweater had come through clearly on the surveillance record. The absence of raised veins indicated youth, possibly a life of ease. The nails were clipped and clean. No identifying rings. The Incoming bracelet appeared to be real copper. The sweater, real wool. Best guess: a crook. Perhaps a wealthy tech smuggler.

"Where did Paco show up next?" Jedda asked. He was sitting in their living room, sipping a fizzy.

"A house near Des Moines," answered Farmer El Din. "He slept and ate and bathed there and dyed his hair. Yellow."

"Even his chest hair!" Mrs. El Din added. "Can you imagine? What madness he has been driven to by that seductive vixen. Our only son! Heir to the biggest corn farm in North Carolina! Throwing his life away for an oversized chantoozy! And don't imagine Big Lizzie isn't capable of violence. The moment our people entered the house, it exploded."

"Your people..." Horatio murmured.

"Thank God only one of our gladiators got hurt and that was just an ear. We had it replaced right away."

Horatio rose from his chair and stood looking out the window at the rustling corn.

"Do you know where Paco is now?"

"No."

"So let's see. You employed private security cameras that could only have been purchased on the black market. You hired private gladiators. Is it possible that you did not know you were breaking the law?"

"We were desperate! Your people haven't been able to stop these kids..."

"And now 'your people' haven't been able to stop them either." He turned toward the El Dins. The sun's glare blanked out his lenses, giving him a terrifying aura of zombie eyelessness. "Two days after the explosion in Des Moines, a sunflight with battery problems made an emergency landing off the Oregon coast. The passengers were observed bobbing on the ocean in their safety boats, Paco among them. He had his violin, his banjo, a particularly lovely instrument which I am told is called an oud, and an antique gypsy tambourine. He also had the most advanced state-of-the-art keyboard that anyone in our Orchestra Coalition has ever seen. Several of the other passengers reported that he was picked up by an ocean-going canoe and disappeared." Jedda sighed; or maybe it was a growl, low in the throat and soft. "Safe houses. Maritime rescues. Expensive instruments, most likely gifts from someone with a keen personal interest in Paco."

Mrs. El Din began to weep.

"Clearly your son has fans. And they have helped him become what he clearly wants to be: an itinerant musician." Horatio's Incoming ejected a disk. "The Corporation has been able to face these facts. Now you must do the same. I have a disk for you to sign."

"I worked my whole life for this land, Jedda," said Farmer El Din. "My boy has to inherit it."

"The law is specific. No one can inherit farmland that he or she does not live on and personally cultivate. Paco has declared publicly and repeatedly that he will never work this land. You are done here."

Mrs. El Din had thrown herself headlong onto the sofa. She was sobbing.

"In this instrument," Jedda continued, "the Corporation commits to giving Paco every assistance to assure his success as a musician. We will equip him with the finest teachers, send him on tour, broadcast his concerts, guarantee his financial security and that of his family, namely you. We will drop all charges against him stemming from the unauthorized song change incident at Dr. Bright's funeral, and we will overlook the crimes against your fellow shareholders to which you have just admitted.

"In exchange you will forfeit your share of this farm to the Corporation. If you don't comply, you will be punished for your crimes and Paco will never work again."

Mrs. El Din had already given up the sobbing thing.

"When you die," she said, "I am going to have a big party."

News of the tragedy that had befallen the El Dins plowed northward through the agroclan gossip lanes. Furlong Burton and his family, alerted to Jedda's impending visit to their farm, expected the worst.

Petunia baked cookies with real eggs. Odin took a bath and combed his sandy hair and put on a clean shirt. Furlong gathered them both into his arms and told them that whatever happened, he loved them, and as long as they had each other, they would be okay.

Athena tried to join them from her glacial exile, ducking under her father's arms to share the group hug. She could almost really feel Furlong's embrace, smell her mother's perfume, kiss her kid brother's grown-up whiskery cheek. Almost really.

Horatio's suncopter landed on the outskirts of the northern hillside field. Flat gray clouds weighed down. There was no wind. He walked slowly, his face in shadow, and the Burtons walked beside him, leaning in to catch his every word.

The problem was, he said, that Furlong's niece Elizabeth had a created a bit of an incident.

"I knew Foxie and Lizzie would get this family into trouble," anguished Petunia. "I knew it. We should never have sent them on vacation."

What with Eddie Bright's refusal to return to the fold, the situation had grown extremely complicated.

"He's not *our* ancestor, you know. Not one gene from that old grouch pollutes our children."

Some Corporation Board members felt extremely put out with the whole Burton Bright clan. They had the sense that the clan could not be trusted.

"But why?! Our branch has nothing to do the NewLA branch! We pay our dues. We turn over our share of every harvest."

It would really help, Horatio continued, if Elizabeth and Eddie could be prevailed upon to behave sensibly, no more incendiary songs, no more of these explosive weather reports that make the Meteorology Department so envious and cranky.

"So," Furlong murmured. "The Meteorology Department. Okay okay."

The Antarctic Germplasm Bank had asked for Elizabeth and her band to make an appearance; so had Professor Mugombo's group at The Sun Project. Horatio was inclined to grant these requests. But Lizzie would have to sing responsibly.

"My dear Athena will speak to her. Lizzie's just a ditsy girl. Athena is the vastly superior intellect. If Athena speaks to her, I'm sure she'll settle down. I'll send her a mes..."

"Mom," Odin said. "The man is offering us a deal. For God's sake, shut up and listen."

Petunia gasped. Furlong smiled.

It would really help, Jedda continued, if Eddie could be convinced to come in from wherever he was hiding and join the Corporate fold once again. If the Burton branch of the clan could produce him, the Board would feel grateful. All the hopes and dreams of the kids in the family would come true. Odin would certainly make gladiator and enjoy a lucrative sporting career before he took over the farm. And Athena would easily win her professorship, the youngest full professor in the history of agrotech, and she would be able to leave that frozen wasteland and come home and teach at the university and invent great miracle foods forever redounding to the honor and profit of her family and her continent.

Just before reboarding his suncopter, Horatio took Furlong aside.

"I'd like to announce Eddie's return in December at a meeting of your Agroclans Society," he said. "Not an 'Incoming Assembly.' A face-to-face. Two hundred people max."

Furlong squinted at him.

"You want a real physical in-the-flesh meeting."

"Yes."

"With 200 people present in the same hall."

"Yes."

"Wow."

"Not completely unprecedented. We had that many for Clyde Bright's funeral. Get it together and you will receive all the EMMY-B-GONE you need, free of charge."

Furlong nodded.

They shook hands.

"I'm not a fan of agro-poisons," Furlong said. "What about resistant seed?"

Something about the farmer's wind-beaten face and calloused hand made Horatio decide to give him an honest answer.

"Not happening as fast as I would like."

"The Past on Pico Two", a small shop on the eastern end of NewLA abutting the western edge of the Mohave Spread, did not try to appear especially inviting. An antique door of real wood hung back between two jutting display windows. In the right window, there was a hand-operated vacuum cleaner of the sort once popular before the Corporation exhaust system started sucking up everybody's dust automatically on Mondays. The left window displayed a lawn mower from the days when many shareholders had green grass growing around their free-standing houses. Only farmers and certain top Corporation leaders lived in such houses today, and they wouldn't dream of giving over even a square yard of productive soil to decorative grass.

An ancient cow bell jangled when Horatio opened the front door. It was about four o'clock. The main business of the day had ended, and Evangeline Corelli was cleaning and straightening her pawed-over stock.

She did not see him enter, although she must have heard the bell. "Come on in," she called. "Feel free to browse. I'll be with you in a moment."

Horatio parked Lizzie's blue suitcase near a stack of ancient cooking pots and used the moment to observe her mother.

Evangeline wore a faded blue suit. Her lenses hung around her neck from a red ribbon. She was a busty, fast-moving woman. Little silver studs in her ears and nose. Compelling eyes like her mother and her daughter. But no style, no affect, aggressively plain. Perhaps a reaction against Foxie's flamboyance, Horatio thought. She reminded him of her father, Eddie Bright. Preoccupied. Important things to think about. No time for fun.

She followed her fake feather duster through the store, whistling some tune. Her pony tail swung like the needle of a metronome.

The sight of the long scar that divided her face recalled to Horatio the Baha raiders leaping from the Pacific sea wall; their blood-curdling screams; their machetes slashing. He wiped his eyes, expelling the vision. Noted the photo of Evangeline in the arms of her towering husband. The legend said "Captain James Corelli. Killed at the Battle of Mendocino Heights. January 2134."

Lizzie was 20 years old now. Born in 2146. And she had been fathered by a man who had been killed 12 years earlier. Obviously Captain Corelli and his wife had saved frozen embryos as insurance against the possibility of death in battle.

Horatio succumbed for a moment to an emotion he despised — envy. No one had saved embryos to continue the Jedda line when he went off to fight.

The stuff in the little store had been left deliberately mixed: real wool blankets with old telephones with table crystal with firearms with assorted furniture for tall people, who had been so much more numerous in the past than today. If you were looking for something specific, say a book printed on paper, you would have to wander among baskets of strange kitchen gadgets, scrubbers and peelers, and music preserved on large discs, ornate mirrors and lamps wired for incandescent bulbs. Scattered through all of it, landscape paintings. Everybody wanted those. Copies of Corots and Monets, California Plein Air ocean vistas and Hudson River School masterpieces with tiny people dwarfed by towering nature. Bygone scenery, triggering the recall of bygone songs. *The green grass is gone from the hill...where once the daisies sprung...* A wise business strategy, he thought, to force customers to pass by items they might never have known they desired.

Evangeline turned a corner and almost smashed into him.

"Sorry. Didn't see you there," she said. "May I help you?"

She was so close to him that she could look directly into his eyes, something he never allowed. Horatio flinched and backed away and turned his head aside as though he had been attacked by a glaring light, even though they were standing in the most shadowy part of the little store. He knew she had recognized him.

"How much for this rocking chair?"

"Three thousand. For you, ten thousand, you son-of-a-bitch."

"My grandfather had one like it."

"Why are you here? What do you want? Haven't you made enough trouble for this family?"

"We ought to talk."

"Get out of my store."

"My suncopter is right outside. Let me take you to dinner in Minnesota at 'Rose'n'Harry's.' They serve actual trout."

"Get out of my store now."

"We ought to talk about Elizabeth. She could have a great future."

"As what? A super model for sizes no one wears? You ruined her future."

"Only temporarily. She was passed over at the Music Talent Auction as a punishment for singing a song that was not authorized by the Corporation. I couldn't just let it go. My colleagues on the Board would never have stood for that. I am sure you understand. However, all this mess can be made right. We can start over. Elizabeth can have the education and the future she wants. We just have to talk about it."

"Why are you so worried about a 20-year old girl?"

"Aren't you worried, Mrs. Corelli? You're her mother. She's out there playing with fire, tempting the wrath of unreasonable people."

"And I suppose you are one of the reasonable ones, Mr. Jedda."

"Dr. Jedda. You bet I am. I am as reasonable as it gets."

He loosened his collar and settled back into the rocking chair and began to rock. She whispered "Damn" because she could see, he was not leaving.

She sat opposite him on a cleared shelf. Inserted her lenses. Crossed her arms over her chest. Her thighs, jammed together, made a tough muscular bulge in her skirt.

He asked: "Do you have other children?"

"No." He didn't press her. He just waited. The store was getting dark. It was twilight. She relented. "I started trying to bring our embryos to term two years after James was killed. Every couple of years, I would try again. I had six possible babies. Lizzie was the last and the only one to make it."

"I am very sorry to hear that."

"She is my everything. I will not let anybody hurt her." Mimicking him, her eyes cold. "I am sure you understand."

"I do."

"What about you? Where are your children?"

149

"When you work in agrotech, you lose the ability to achieve certain things."

"But why would you settle for that? Why wouldn't you look for a fatherless kid and adopt?"

"To not be vulnerable. To have no soft spot," he said, wondering why he felt so compelled to be truthful to Foxie's children.

Evangeline laughed. "God, you people are crazy."

"No. Not crazy. Just interested in power. Somebody has got to be in power, Mrs. Corelli, even in a pretty fair and equitable shareholding system like ours. Just because we don't believe that leaders should be celebrities does not mean we don't believe in leadership. Somebody has to organize the continent's priorities, in the hope of eventually restoring even a little of what has been lost."

Evangeline sighed; slipped off her shoe; rubbed her tired foot.

"I don't know where Daddy is. Or Lizzie. I gather you don't know where they are either, so that's a relief. What do you want?"

"A contract. Same as we make with our scientists. With Felicity Bjornsdottir, for example, who has been mentoring your niece Athena. With Stevie Foster, who invented the wheat that grows in your brother's fields. A contract to share the profit from Eliza...Lizzie's music."

"Are you kidding? You expect there to be profit?"

"Oh yes."

"And what if she isn't interested? What if she'd rather take her chances as an independent, playing live concerts, no Corporation broadcasts, no Beam..."

"It won't work, Evangeline. The Corporation has too much control. Your family is too vulnerable on too many fronts." She laughed defiantly. But he wouldn't stop. "How's about this? I will authorize Professor Bjornsdottir to invite Lizzie and her band to perform at the germplasm bank. If she sings the right songs there, I promise you, I will send her on to The Sun Project, and then bring her home, to entertain at the Agroclans Society meeting in December.

"The Corporation will broadcast her concerts. Uncut. Applause and all. The Bloomington Music School will rescind its rejection and snap her up. She'll be on her way to becoming a legitimate, well-paid Beamstar."

"Her new clothes were stolen."

"They're in a suitcase by your front door."

She regarded him with sympathy.

"Aren't you ashamed of yourself? A big shot like you, so frightened of an old man and a young girl."

"No. I am not ashamed. I am indeed frightened of Lizzie. And especially frightened of your father. I lie awake nights trying to figure out how to lure them in from the cold, to make them part of us again. But there are others in the Corporation who are not as frightened as I am. And if you don't make a deal with me, you will have to deal with them. And as you have seen, they don't offer to take you to dinner and discuss things in a reasonable manner. They shoot and even when they miss, they do terrible damage."

He was looking directly at her. Evangeline had seen this man making his speech on The Beam, but not until now did his features actually come into focus. She noticed that he wore sprays of faint scars around each eye and each ear and across his nose, evidence that these were not originals but replacements.

She wondered in which battle he had lost his face.

The sun had set. The only artificial light in "The Past on Pico Two" was the steady light of the Incoming embedded on the back of the man's left hand. Evangeline unlocked her arms and relaxed her legs. She clasped her hands behind her neck and leaned back on them. She said: "If you're taking me to dinner, and we're going to eat trout together, and we're going to talk seriously, I would like some privacy. Are you important enough to get that thing turned off?"

Instead of languishing in little jars capped with their names and dates, the ashes of many starved children had been dug into the earth of Corporate vegetable gardens. For every child, a real tomato or pepper or cucumber could be planted. For groups of siblings, you could have vines – eggplants, beans, zucchini. If you wanted to keep remembering, you could pay for a new vegetable to be planted every year. Most plants didn't make it, weather and soil conditions having become what they were. If the plant survived, you could take home 15% of the yield.

Many people gave up after a while. Once the wars had ended and the Corporation had begun feeding everybody adequately, there were living children to worry about.

Foxie did not give up. She did not forget. She poked her spade, loosening the soil around Frankie, now a plum tomato, and cleared off the little plaque beneath the small scarlet fruit. *Franklin, March 12, 2069 – August 17, 2069.* She sprinkled a tiny pouch of tea leaves onto Maddy, now a cluster of pale green peppers. *Madeline, May 21, 2064 – June 5, 2065.* They were bones when they died, little bunches of bones in her hands, and she sure as hell was not going to let them be lost like the other millions upon millions who fertilized the earth without memorial.

She sat between the two markers. She pressed the names and dates of her vanished babies into the crumbled soil and watered it with her tears.

Esmerelda Wolf did not disturb her. The tall, iron-faced woman did not forget how famine took the children first. You could be pretty sure that a woman of 120 or so like Foxie had buried some kids when she was young. If she was lucky, she stayed fertile long enough to give birth to a couple of replacements. Then when they grew up, she had to hold her breath again as they marched off to war.

Esmerelda hung back in a grove of almost-dead cherry trees named for a school of teenage boys. She waited for Foxie to dry her eyes and repair her make-up.

"Mrs. Burton Bright..."

"What is it?! What has happened?!"

"Nothing is wrong. I wished only to speak with you."

"You scared the shit out of me. Do you always sneak up on people like that?"

"Yes."

"I've seen you before."

"I am Esmerelda Wolf. I work for Horatio Jedda. He has sent me to give you a message."

"What? Another deal? My kids told me all about your Mr. Jedda's visits."

"Dr. Jedda."

"Can't you just give it a rest?"

"No," Esmerelda said. "Now consider this. The Corporation offers amnesty to Eddie Bright. Complete amnesty. All charges dropped as though they never existed. Total rehabilitation. A new job as senior Beam weatherman, with his own staff, his choice, salary and benefits to be negotiated, but you can be sure Dr. Jedda has every intention of being generous."

Foxie laughed. "Look around you, lady. Do you see any trust bushes growing here?" She walked up close to Esmerelda and peered into her hard, still face. "What's wrong with you people? Why are you so expressionless? Your faces don't move, your eyes have no light...are you some secret kind of robots or something?"

"I lost my face in the coastal wars. So did Dr. Jedda. This face was the best that battlefield medicine could manage at that time. Your daughter was luckier. She escaped with a scar."

Foxie backed off, appalled and guilty. "Of course. God. I'm sorry."

"The Agrotech Division wants its best weatherman back."

"My Frankie's father drowned. My Maddy's father died of the flu. My Furlong's father was shot dead while trying to distribute food to hungry people. And now you want me to trust the Corporation with the life of my last man, the father of my Evangeline, a man the Corporation tried to murder at his own brother's funeral!"

Esmerelda took a breath. How she wished that Horatio had heeded her advice and cleaned out that whole bloodthirsty, incompetent enclave instead of just disappearing the few who had ordered Eddie's death.

"That was a rogue operation. The perpetrators are no longer with us."

Foxie sagged onto a stone bench. The flesh around her jawbone showed a tiny bit of slack.

Esmerelda sat beside her. She had been reading security reports about the Burton-Bright-Corelli clan for years. She felt as though she knew them, as though if she had a family, if *only* she had a family, they might be hers. She imagined them gathered around the Burtons' kitchen table, which she had seen so often on surveillance discs. The good-natured, sweaty jock Odin, the brilliant Athena with her stash of lovers, the glamorous Petunia and the no-nonsense Evangeline, and Furlong, with his broad-brimmed farmer's hat, presiding over all of it, and Foxie playing the piano, singing duets with her protégé, the tuneful, frolicsome Lizzie, and Eddie Bright, rocking in the rocking chair, smoking his pipe, waiting patiently for great grandchildren... It was such a beautiful picture.

"All Eddie has to do is walk out of his hiding place," she said softly. "Send his people home, no retribution, no danger. Just plain peace. You can be together again, a family again. A whole big healthy clan, Foxie. With generations. With children's children. That is so rare in this world. And you have built it, with your strength of mind and your talent, your good looks and your good luck. Why sacrifice such an achievement for one fleeting moment of free speech?" Esmerelda took her hand. "Please. Bring Eddie home. Just bring him home. We need him. Think of Lizzie. She will be a Beamstar, like you were. She and her band will be famous and beloved, and all your family will be safe."

15. The hissing winds lifted up EMMY...

*T*he hissing winds lifted up EMMY, along with tons of precious topsoil, spinning her around and around until she couldn't tell where she was any more.

She had planned to winter over in Armenia and then fly north to infect millions of hectares of delicious Russian wheat in the spring. But when the winds finally let her settle, she found herself back in China.

Not a bad outcome for EMMY, since the drought days had ended, and it was cool, raining lightly before dawn, and the Chinese farmers had just seeded their fields.

EMMY waited for the plants to sprout and mature just a little. Then she attacked.

Clouds of deadly fungicide rose up to meet her. She died by the trillions of trillions.

The slaughter had been enabled by a Chinese goat robot – the one who had **not** lost his footing in Mongolia -- who had plucked samples of EMMY-infected Waco wheat out of the mountains. These had been used to develop an EMMY-specific poison, similar to the one developed by the North Americans. But the Chinese pellets had not eight but ten sides, and each side could protect not just 100 but 300 acres.

Some of EMMY's spores reached for a breeze and tried to fly away. But the breeze was pathetic; a breath; a sigh.

She sought shelter among the feathers of a shambling old duck. But the feathers were full of fungicide.

If only some rain would come and wash her out of these killer fields and onto the outlying meadows. If only she could hide there in one of those dark red bushes with the little scarlet berries...

16. THE EMMY TOUR

The directive on my Incoming shocked us all.
WE ARE SENDING YOU AND YOUR ENSEMBLE ON WHAT WILL NOW BE KNOWN AS **"The EMMY Tour"**, TO ENTERTAIN THE GALLANT SHAREHOLDERS LABORING TO PROTECT US AGAINST THE ONCOMING WHEAT PLAGUE. ALL PAST CONFLICTS BETWEEN US ARE FORGOTTEN. YOUR HONORS WILL BE REINSTATED. YOUR FAMILIES WILL BE COMPENSATED. YOUR CONCERTS WILL BEAM LIVE TO A LARGE SELECTED AUDIENCE. YOU WILL BE OUR NEW TROUBADOURS. CONGRATULATIONS.

As usual, Grandpa said I was a naïve fool for even listening to such baloney. But Sunshine's sister called to say her extra rations and all his medals and awards had been restored. And Paco's father called to say: "You're all we've got now, boy. Do us proud." (Paco's mother would not speak to him.)

Then Mom called. "Yes. Go. It's okay. Your clothes have been returned, not touched, tags still on. They'll be waiting for you in Antarctica. Go ahead. Sing for the people."

We took a vote and decided, three to one, to take a chance and accept The EMMY Tour.

AT THE ANTARCTIC GERMPLASM BANK

Like Grandpa, Willy, our *"No"* vote, was sure we were being bamboozled and betrayed. Every time our Corporate sunflight hit some rough air, he cried "I knew it! *Nous sommes perdus!*"

We landed on a glacier. Hunks of snow-covered ice poked up from it. One of the hunks turned into the germplasm bank's tippy top turret. The other hunks were hunks of snow-covered ice.

With a whoosh, the turret rose up in front of us and became a high wide white tower. We were loaded onto a hoversled that raced down an iceway. The iceway led to a door in the tower. The door opened and we slid right through. An optical shield dropped over us. Armed men in white uniforms surrounded us.

"So it is to being a trap after all," Willy cried. "*Au revoir, mes enfants!* Wherever you end, remembering the advice of the great Sinatra: always to pronouncing the final consonant."

Doors closed behind us. We were carried downward. Other doors opened in front of us. The optical shield melted away. We stepped off the sled. All the employees of the germplasm bank, in their pink and blue and lavender lab coats, had gathered to meet us.

Professor Bjornsdottir (looking like a sofa in a cream-colored caftan printed all over with green vines) announced: "Ladies and gentlemen, I give you (reading from a list) Lizzie Corelli, Paco El Din, Willy Sachertorte and Sunshine Gomez! Le Tall Band! Surprise!"

The crowd shouted with astonishment and burst into applause. I realized that the professor had told no one about our arrival. We were a special treat. The EMMY Tour was for real.

My cousin Athena flew into my arms.

It was absolutely amazing how lousy Athena looked. Her rosy face had gone seriously pale. Her big blue eyes were buried in dark clouds. She wore a tight fitting white anti-bacterial hat over her curls. Her lab coat was actually dirty. A deep vertical worry wrinkle had settled between her eyebrows.

She took me on a tour of the bank. I had to slow down to keep up with her. I mean, Athena was really dragging.

Each floor had a big cheerful lab, lit with so much stored sunlight that you actually felt like you were outdoors. The office cubicles, cozy and warm, were connected by glass corridors lit from within by pretty colored lights that changed constantly, kind of like an interior aurora borealis. The food was served in halls painted up to look like the tropical paradises there used to be when there used to be Tahiti and Florida.

Athena said Professor Bjornsdottir did everything possible to relieve the pressure on her workers. She offered poetry readings, hula lessons, casino nights where you could gamble with nuts and pits, glass blowing demonstrations, gladiators doing synchronized acrobatics. She encouraged romantic entanglements, maintaining that sex kept people from going crazy. (Although amazingly, Athena herself didn't seem to have a current boyfriend.)

The professor played music non-stop. "Even the newest songs," Athena said. "And she won't pay. She just won't. She says music is a necessary medical expense needed to energize people, like daily vitamins. This is going to bring us trouble. I know it. I just know it."

I had the feeling that, despite Professor Bjornsdottir's best efforts to dress up this underground icebox, Athena was still going nuts in it.

She leaned toward me, whispering. "This is the Corporation's best guarded facility. We've got ordermen prowling the perimeters 24-7. If you approach our turret without the right lenses, you won't see the purple lines that mark our borders, and if you step over them, you'll be disintegrated. If your entry physical doesn't check out with the turret sensors, a drone bullet with your name on it tranquilizes you, seals you up in a security bubble and carries you off for questioning. They never fail to get you to tell them what they want to know."

"Oh come on, Miss Baloney Pants, you're just trying to scare me."

"You know this stem rust plague..."

"The one that Dr. Jedda was talking about on The Beam?"

"Correct. Her name is EMMY. She took out a whole Mongolian harvest in a couple of weeks. Nobody can tell where she is going to show up next."

"Some people think she doesn't exist," I said. "Every day on the weather report, Arliss laughs and calls her 'Jedda's Folly'."

"That imbecile. Who would believe what he says?"

"Gazillions of people, Theenie. He's a super Beamstar."

"God save us from popular culture," she said. "We're all working day and night to find some genes that can stop EMMY before she goes any further. All home leaves have been cancelled. You and the band, you're the first visitors we've had in months." She gripped my hand. "What if EMMY blows east and crosses the Pacific, Lizzie? What if she gets to Daddy's farm?"

"You're all geniuses here," I said. "You'll stop her. I know you will."

"We're getting nowhere, just nowhere."

"You should go to the infirmary,"

"Many of us believe we should give up and go home. But the bosses won't let us. They persist in their vain hopes."

"You should ask for some pills to help you with the stress."

She pulled me close and whispered. "If you admit to feeling stressed, they don't send you home, which would be wonderful, oh no, they send you to be evaluated by a committee of shrinkers, and they give you shots that make you think you're happy even though you have actually been vegetized, your brain has been slowed down to a useless trot and you can't get any work done and all your colleagues give up on you and your career is over. Or even worse, they send you away to a Corporate recovery center the way they sent Professor Bjornsdottir, and who knows if you will ever come back from there or what you will be like if and when you do? So you can't be stressed. You have to be fine all the time.

"I am fine, Lizzie. I am just fine."

Athena took me to the sweatsy room. They all go every day at the germplasm bank. It's mandatory. We stretched out on the warm boards. Driblets began to run down my scalp into my hair. The muscles in my back began to unclench. I might have dozed off, except that Athena removed her hat.

Her beautiful curls had been totally chopped.

"Why?!"

"Too much trouble. I'm too busy to care about my hair."

"If Grandma heard you say that, she would die of shame."

"How can you stand being with that silly woman? All she cares about is appearances."

"That's not true. She cares about history. Family. And politics."

Athena gave me a sharp look. Her eyes narrowed, her nose lengthened. I was reminded that she was Aunt Petunia's daughter.

"A word of warning, Lizzie. Don't let Grandma get you involved in politics. You're not smart enough to go there."

I was so hurt, I actually couldn't speak for a minute.

Get a grip. Don't let her make you feel bad. You're not thirteen. The pimples are gone. You're not the lesser cousin any more.

"Gee Theenie, I didn't realize you had so much contempt for me."

"There's a big difference between having talent and having brains. Confuse the two and you could get yourself into real trouble. Try and make an effort to learn from your own history. You sang the wrong song at a funeral, and blew your chance to go to music school. Now you are the chick singer in a pick-up band composed of two runaways and a has-been. You're only here because my mother promised Dr. Jedda you would behave yourself and sing the right songs."

"Your mother promised what?!"

"If you screw up this deal, believe me, Lizzie, you will have no future just no future in music."

I stood up. For the first time in my life, I felt glad to be taller than Athena.

"Now you listen to me, you arrogant snot. The Corporation did not send us here because Aunt Petunia made promises. We are here because we are well-known and popular and we have fans!"

"You only have your so-called 'fans' because the agents of the Caliph are grabbing your rehearsals out of the air and using them to interrupt important shows on The Beam. You are being exploited by our enemy competitors!"

I guess we must have been shouting, because the other women in the sweatsy room were telling us to shut up.

"They took the El Din family's land, Lizzie. They could take ours tomorrow. Our clan could lose everything. For God's sakes, stop behaving like such an empty-headed, egotistical jerk and just sing what you're supposed to sing."

In the end, I did let Athena upset me...but not until nobody was around to see. Old, familiar self-hate tears bubbled up at the base of my throat. I tried to swallow them. I tried to wash them off my face with ice cold water. I did calisthenics to shake them loose. But I just couldn't disengage from the feeling that I was a big stupid nothing, that being able to sing was simply a minor trait that had checked in with my DNA, and really, I had achieved exactly zip.

Grandpa's voice said *idiot.*

Athena's voice said *jerk.*

Then Nikolai's voice said *You have the power. You had the courage to sing what you knew those people needed to hear.*

The tears backed down out of my throat.

My cool returned.

I went to rehearsal.

"Listen fellas," I said to my band. "These people here, they're tense and pressured and over-worked. They need fun and comfort songs. Nothing edgy or disturbing. 'Ragtime Band.' 'Four Foot Two.' They need to know we appreciate what they are doing to save us from starvation."

I did not say: "My cousin has warned me that we must prove to the Corporation that our band is not a danger to society."

Screw my stuck-up cousin. I knew how to handle this.

At the concert, I made sure we sneaked a surprise verse into the great public favorite "Miss Betsy from Pike", special for the germplasm bank.

When Betsy was crossing the prairie one night,
She tangled with EMMY, the wheat's farmer's blight,
She called in the seed bank and when they were done,
Red EMMY was returned to OH-blivv-ee-unn!

Sure, it was silly, but it was still a moment of recognition and tribute that the workers there really needed. The crowd went crazy. Felicity was particularly thrilled.

"Incredible! Fabulous! I never thought of that! *You're not a scientist!* You can make up your own material! Why you could even send messages! Boy oh boy, what a piece of luck!"

It's amazing how, when she's focused and excited about something, she can all of a sudden stop stuttering.

"It was just a little joke verse, Professor, no big d…"

"Stop! You must remember this, Lizzie. Excessive humility is unbecoming in an accomplished woman. Come to my office tomorrow. I want to show you a letter."

I had heard of letters. In high school history, they were always talking about how this one wrote to that one and that one wrote to someone else and all those "wrote to's" were letters. I knew there was a postal service in ancient times with private mail in sealed envelopes. And I had seen letters under glass in the museum. But to actually get right up close to a real written letter, well, that would be an experience.

This letter of Felicity's was written by an ancient plant hunter. She had found it tucked among other papers in something she called The Chilean File and had kept it, she admitted, for her own private inspiration.

The letter had never been sent. It was a draft, with stuff crossed out and revised, written in ink on a thin blue paper that folded into its own envelope. It was addressed to the plant hunter's mother. Dated March 1998. Felicity had ordered a translation from the Spanish.

"Mother dear, You always taught us that the bounty of the earth belongs to everyone. That everybody has the right to eat.

But I fear that if things continue as they are now, eating will soon be a privilege. The shortsightedness of the people appears to be bottomless. They ignore the signals of angry nature. Soon a few companies, only a very few, will control the seed supply of the whole world. The bounty of the earth will be chained up, and our children's children will be cast down into hunger and subjugation. I protest, I shout, I make trouble, but I cannot change things, and then I plunge into melancholy and lose my way. I am so sorry not to have been able to change things, Mother."

How terrific it would be, I thought, if I could write a letter like that to my mother, letting her know how much I loved her, and how much I really appreciated all the things she had taught me and how she had suffered to save my life and apologizing for all the things I would not become, so she could hear my true feelings and understand me better than she would ever be able to from our fleeting fighting exchanges.

What an amazing thing. A letter.

I thanked Felicity. I hugged her. Luckily my long arms could reach all the way around. She hugged me back. I can still recall the sweet soft fleshy pressure of her embrace.

The last words she ever said to me were "Do not be silenced or censored, Lizzie. Do not be afraid. You are powerful enough to change things."

THE SUN PROJECT

Nikolai's village lay spread out on a long white table. It looked like dirt. Itamar smoothed it with his graceful, skinny fingers. He blew on it to separate the dust from the more substantial pieces, then ordered his lenses to take a look.

Billions of organisms wriggled and jiggled there, gorging on sub-atomic particles of extinct food, navigating molecular hills and trails. The microscope's ancillary analyzers announced the presence of fossilized falcon eggs, juniper, newsprint, petroleum, the bones of Nikolai's father, blue pine, aluminum, rayon, rhododendron, chicken feathers, bullet shavings, alpine violets, peach pits, plastics (about which Nikolai had only heard legends), the teeth and hair of his sisters and his mother's jade beads. They found goat antler, yak feces, barley, river silt, *ocean* silt, all still detectable years, even eons after their time in the visible world.

For weeks, Nikolai and Itamar examined every trace of every substance in Nikolai's box. And on the fourth day of the fourth week, they found the germ cells of what might possibly once have been the purple wheat called Lucky Boy.

Itamar's biochembots saved a few of the cells and set the rest into dishes of culturing medium. They fed the dishes with minerals, hormones, soil enzymes, a different cocktail devised by Itamar for every group of cells. Most of the cell groups just disappeared. A few began to multiply, clustering new cells around themselves, differentiating as they grew into all the parts that were needed to make a seed.

Itamar ordered Nikolai to work in a remote subsection of a glass house that was allocated to dangerous high hazard sowings, with orders to plant the seed (*will it grow to maturity?*) and then to harvest the seed and plant it again (*will its seed in turn produce viable grain?*) and again and again until there were enough seedlings for an experimental crop.

"Work in silence," said Itamar. He did not look at the young man. He was leaning over his mighty lenses, preoccupied by their world view. "No music. Work when the others are sleeping. No one will try to come in because they all know that's a maximum security unit, which deals with alien germplasm that could pollute the plants the Corporation has engineered. Go now. Get to work."

The absent, casual manner of this directive, its way of preempting further discussion, irritated Nikolai.

"If I may say, sir, is it possible you could be underestimating the danger of what you are suggesting? In China, breeding unauthorized plants is punishable by disappearance."

"Hmmm yes yes. Here in North America as well."

"Once you have the seedlings, what will you do with them?"

"I will infect them with EMMY."

"And if they die…"

"I will look for resistance elsewhere. Perhaps in another species…"

"And if they survive…"

"Enough questions for now, Nicholas."

"It's Nikolai."

Still concentrating on his work, still not looking at Nikolai, Itamar said "Yes yes by all means. Nikolai. I apologize."

"Now that you have excavated my village and found your treasure, I want all the territory restored to its coffin. Please order the agrobots to do that immediately so I may go to my post with the coffin in my possession. "

Nikolai's harsh tone finally made Itamar straighten up and pay attention. In the Himalayan kid's hard, narrow black eyes, he found an alarming measure of hostility.

"No need for so much concern, my boy."

"I must be the judge of that. Sir."

Itamar wondered what had possessed Stevie Foster to saddle him with such a fierce assistant.

Nikolai carried the coffin through the corridors to his secret glass house unit. His leg hurt. His hand hurt. His face, healing, itched unbearably.

He didn't trust Itamar Mugombo. Found him vague, not plain spoken, slippery as a silverfish. He knew that he had been drawn into a plot to capture a buried landrace wheat variety, which Nikolai Vavilov had once found and the world had subsequently lost. He knew that the retrieved Tibetan germplasm might contain an EMMY barrier. However, he wasn't quite sure how the great discovery would be used and for whose benefit.

Despite his respect and affection for Professor Foster, he did not particularly like the way his participation in this caper had been mandated without his prior consent. *Whatever job he gives you, that's the right job for you. Just do what he says…*

He was no longer quite as impressed with his mentors as he had been last year. He had his own ideas about who should profit from the conquest of EMMY.

In only a few months, Nikolai had raised a couple of handfuls of viable Lucky Boy seed.

He kept one handful for his own purposes. He planted the other.

And one day, just at noon, when the whole Sun Project snored, he limped through the hot corridors and presented Itamar Mugombo with exactly 144 healthy greenish purple sprouts.

Itamar put the biochembots to sleep. Enveloped the lab in a security seal. Doused the seedlings with EMMY.

He and Nikolai waited.

Itamar bowed his head in prayer.

Nikolai watched him with cold suspicion.

Images of what was going on inside the wheat at that moment rose up around them. They stood inside the plants, locked in like observers at an execution.

As it had in the St. Paul lab, the red invader beat on the cell walls of the healthy wheat. Poked and banged, looking for a soft spot. Bounced off. Tried again. Tried again. Bounced off again.

They waited a week and re-did the entire experiment from scratch, with an entirely different batch of EMMY.

She assailed the Lucky Boy sprouts with her usual vigor. Poke. Poke. Bang. Bang. She did not retreat, but she did not succeed.

Itamar showed no excitement.

He ran the experiment again and yet again, each time with a different batch of EMMY.

Lucky Boy held fast every time.

They had a winner.

Itamar immediately notified the other two Grain Guardians as well as Horatio Jedda that unfortunately, his latest effort in the search for a wheat with genes that would resist EMMY had failed.

Nikolai slipped behind him and held the Chinese knife across his throat.

"You are sending out a lie. Why?"

"Oh sweet Lord, I knew it, I could feel it, I knew you were an assassin."

"You are hiding my family's wheat from Dr. Foster and Professor Bjornsdottir. Why?"

"It's a code, you fool. They know I'm lying."

"Don't ever call me a fool, Mugombo. Does Jedda know you are lying?"

"No."

"The Corporation pays you, pays for this lab, this research, and rightfully expects to own 85% of our discovery, and you are stealing it."

"They own too much! It cannot possibly be right, for a few people to control the seed and all its generations. This owning has gone too far. It has spread like an infection from the plants to the people, and now we are all owned, Nikolai, and the next generation will be owned too, talent brains muscle everything we have by nature will be owned, and if we want to stop the generation after that from being owned, we must act now. Oh please do not kill me. It has taken us so many years to amass the courage to do this. Stevie said I could trust you."

"He said I could trust you too. But he is an innocent person, and perhaps you have decided he is a fool as well, and you are just using him. Who are you stealing for? Are you working for the Caliph? The tech smugglers? The Chinese?"

"Please..."

"God help you if you are working for the Chinese."

"No no, that's not it, I swear!"

"I am not one of your eternally grateful young pirates, Professor. You cannot use me as a field hand the way you use these sad little whores. Tell me the truth or I will cut out your throat. Who are you working for?"

The exquisitely honed blade sent a trickle of blood rolling down Itamar's neck. He could only manage to croak: "I am working for the commons."

"Who is that?"

"It is us, Nikolai. All of us."

Le Tall Band flew into the Mohave Spread at night. To me, it felt like flying over water, because the whole sky, the moon and the stars and the cascading space debris, even our sunflight itself, was reflected in the array of solar collectors below us. Thousands of miles wide and long, the array wound through the southwest on pathways that, our hoverride told us, had been cleared originally for ancient military bases.

Professor Mugombo had completely forgotten that we were coming.

He emerged from his lab flustered and befuddled. "Ah yes yes, the musicians. By all means come in. I apologize for my absent-mindedness. Welcome."

His assistants quickly made up our rooms and settled us in. We wanted to go to sleep. But nobody sleeps at night in The Sun Project.

I was excited.

Grandma had called, saying that the germplasm bank concert had been broadcast on The Beam, and the word on the street was that our pertinent viewers loved us.

Mom reported that the Bloomington Music School had sent a delegation to see her personally to say their rejection had resulted from an unfortunate clerical error, they were very sorry and would be delighted to have me as their student.

"What did you say to them?"

"I said when Elizabeth returns from her world tour, we might possibly discuss their offer."

She laughed. She looked strangely young. Even pretty. Her pony tail was bouncing.

"What's going on, Mom?"

"Same old same old."

"Tell me the truth. Something's going on."

"Whatever they pay you for these concerts, I expect to receive enough of it to retile the store and repair the humidifying system."

All the work at The Sun Project is done before nine in the morning and after five in the afternoon. In between, the people eat and sleep. For recreation, they have table games, a couple of gyms, a non-fiction library, one really amazing concert grand piano and some meditation alcoves.

Dr. Mugombo is no Dr. Bjornsdottir.

He told us that Sun Project workers can't be younger than 12 or older than 28. They operate according to Dr. Jedda's policy of limited collegiality, never spending more than one year with one crew so they don't become more attached to each other than to their work.

I wondered, now that we were back in the good graces of the Corporation, if Paco and Sunshine and Willy and I would be allowed to stay together long enough to develop our style and our repertoire, or if we'd soon be farmed out to other music groups whether we liked it or not.

Happy as I was about our new status, there were things I thought about now that had never occurred to me before.

Maybe I should try to tweak this deal.

Maybe I needed an agent.

Professor Mugombo took us around the campus.

First we met the scorpion herds. God, what a horrible sight that was, all those hideous creatures with their poison fangs, prowling in their cages, *scratch scratch*, nibbling crickets. The herds were managed by entomologists but handled by robots. Each robot had long metal arms, with special pouches where the scorpions could sting and deposit their venom. When the arms were loaded up, they would amputate themselves into a bin where they would be picked up by other robots who would collect the venom.

The guys in the band found all this fascinating. I found it revolting. Two minutes and I was out of there.

The greenhouse workers got started at midnight. They adjusted the temperature and humidity to make a perfect atmosphere for whatever was being grown and shuffled around, clipping and cultivating by the light of their hats under simulated moonlight until morning, when the sunshine lights gradually came on like a real dawn. Then the workers packed the hats away and began talking to their plants.

So it was true, what the fan at the funeral had said: Professor Mugombo does actually believe in talking to the plants.

We followed him through his convoluted maze of glass houses. In one of them, gangs of teensy trees were growing. He said that with the help of certain bees and wasps, which he was raising in a buzzing anteroom - *Did I want to see them? Thanks, but maybe another time.* - they would someday bear a flavorful nut once known as "allmounds." In another greenhouse, vines bearing melons made of sweet pink juice twined on jets of mist. In another, we saw roses. Real perfumesy roses, in yellow and gold and pink and all shades of red.

Girls around my age cared for the roses, spritzing, clipping and all the while talking to the plants. *Hi there, Versailles. How's about a little drink? I know it's brackish water but it's all we've got.* Nothing serious; just a kind of constant schmooze.

"What do you do with all these beautiful flowers, Professor?"

"Some go to the Personal Products Division to perfume soaps and cosmetics. Others become homes for useful insects. Often we just grow them so we can look at them and smell them. Like your songs, young lady. They simply make us happy."

He wandered on ahead, murmuring to the yellow teas.

One of the girls - Nammsie, she called herself; short for Vietnam, now gone under the sea - told me that Professor Mugombo had raised the roses from microscopic specks of their ancestors that used to grow here years ago before it was desert. "The truth is, he doesn't just grow them for fun," she explained. "He uses the roses as currency. He re-did the kitchen with them.

And bought our piano. He sacrificed the grandifloras to ransom me and a bunch of my friends off the brothel ship. He's still paying. Every week, three dozen get delivered to the madam."

I guess I couldn't handle that one. Must've looked shocked.

Nammsie laughed at me. "You rich North American girls, you really don't know shit."

At 9:30 in the morning, everybody said goodbye to the scorpions and the greenhouses and returned to headquarters. In an hour, the whole Sun Project was fed and bedded down for the hottest part of the day.

The guys in the band went right to sleep. Not me. I kept thinking of this singer I had once met at "Foxie's, Where Dinner Comes a'Singing." She wasn't really there, of course; she was just an interactive from the 20th century. She sang the blues and wore flowers in her hair. I mean, she would have been the same great singer even if she wore nothing in her hair. But the flowers added style and beauty.

I thought Professor Mugombo and his assistants wouldn't mind if I took some of the roses, not a grandiflora because those had to be saved for the madam, but maybe a spray of little climbers, bright red, just one little stem... to give me some confidence for tonight's concert...because first Grandpa and then Athena and now Nammsie had made me feel so dumb and out of touch...and I needed to believe Professor Bjornsdottir that I wasn't just some mindless entertainer, that I was actually an accomplished woman and had something to offer the world, like Miss Holiday.

So around midday, I tiptoed back through the tunnels into the greenhouses. Even with the filters and the cooling systems, it was really hot. I said Hi to the plants I passed in accordance with the custom of the country, heading for the roses. And wouldn't you know, I got lost.

I found myself in a grove of pungent trees labeled "youcalipptus." White birds cooed in the branches.

I wandered into a steamy compost room where disgusting worms crawled, and the stench made you want to throw up.

I pushed open a door and arrived in a cold bright place filled wall-to-wall with pots of purplish-green rustling grass.

I stood there, totally turned around and directionless, feeling like the superfool that my detractors thought I was.

Directly in front of me, like they were guarding the grass, sat these cages, balanced on rickety tables and filled with scorpions.

A shrieking raptor came swooping down from the rafters, heading for my eyes. I screamed and dropped to the floor and wriggled under one of the tables.

Somebody yelled "Ludmilla! Go back to your eggs!"

The raptor re-ascended and sat on her nest, glaring. Above my head, the scorpions scratched.

I could hear the man walking toward me. He tapped a cane ahead of each step. I was scared to death to come out from under the table and just as scared to stay where I was.

"You are not supposed to be in this section," the man growled. He sounded very angry. "No one is allowed to enter. The whole place could be infected."

I called out: "I'm sorry I'm sorry! I didn't mean to disturb! I got lost! I was only looking for a flower!"

Nikolai crouched down. He had grown a moustache. He looked older.

"There is only one flower here," he said.

He pulled me to him and kissed me. I felt dizzy. Lost my balance. I put my hands up into his sleeves and felt his arms and tasted his teeth and his neck. God, he is such a magic guy for me.

The jets opened and soaked us and the scorpions and all the little wheat plants they were guarding with mist.

I told Paco and Sunshine and Willy: "Many of the people here come from hard lives. Like really terrible lives. Now they're stuck herding scorpions and chatting up flowers. They can never go outside and run around and play in the sun. Mugombo's idea of a fun game is checkers. So I think we should get them dancing."

Professor Mugombo decreed a night off. Everybody in The Sun Project gathered at seven o'clock in the central common room.

Paco played the opening to the "Brindisi" from *La Traviata*, on single keys, very slowly, and then *pow!* the lights came up and we rocked on with Sunshine's drums and Willy on the trombone and me singing in my chest voice and shaking my tambourine and wearing my roses. I don't think that was the way the song was meant to be sung, but nobody there except maybe Willy and Professor Mugombo had ever heard the original, so we did what we thought was best. By the end everybody was jiving and jumping and raising hell and nobody sat down for the rest of the night. We played rhumbas and polkas and old-time rock and roll. We did "Oleana" as a floor-busting hora. The walls shook. Chairs broke. Wine spilled. Somebody got mad and hit somebody and there was a huge free-for-all brawl with many minor injuries. Nobody went to bed on time and nobody could get up and go to work the following evening.

Sometimes a person just needs a little tenderness – *I have been dreaming of you. I dream of your blue locket and your blue eyes and your beautiful voice* – to make her feel absolutely sure she can bring down the house.

It was our second night in his narrow bed in his room at the end of the scorpion corridor. Nikolai had made me tired and a little sore, and his sweat was salty on my lips. I felt him shrinking down, listened to his breathing slow. We both needed to sleep for a while. When I woke up, I was lying on my side with my head on his shoulder, and his arms were around me.

The room was labeled as a utility closet, but you could see, many kids had been hidden here. The remnants of their stuff cluttered the shelves. Totems and bead bracelets and single socks and music discs and story discs and really ancient books made of paper and written not with words but with pictures, the kind of books my mother keeps in protective cases in "The Past on Pico Two." The books were battered from so many people using them. I guess Itamar had left them in the room to give the kids something to distract them while hiding, to calm their fears and help them sleep.

"Now let us see what we have here," Nikolai said, turning back the torn cover. I pulled myself up next to him. It was a Chinese book, with pastel drawings of magic places under the sea inhabited by wiggledy creatures, lovely smiling fishes and tentacled octopussies and squarish plankton that looked like transparent floating napkins

My lover held me in his right arm. With his rebuilt left hand, he held the book and read to me, translating as he read.

"Once there was a handsome pink coral reef named Cho Cho who grew like a great forest under the ocean. He had caves and bays and nooks and neighborhoods. And deep inside one of those pretty caves, there lived a little squid named Lulu."

I closed my eyes. This is how I would have felt if my father had lived to read to me.

"Since Lulu had so many hands, she could gather lots of food to keep in her cave. 'We must save up in case of hard times,' she said to Cho Cho. 'For they are sure to come.'"

I reached down and ran my fingers along the seams that held Nikolai's leg together. He was only four years older than I was, but he had met with hard times I had never dreamed of. Me, I was all good fortune and happy songs. Rich North American girl.

"When the storms tore up the seas and the seas grew hot and filled with chemicals, the terrible red algae invaded. They ate up all the oxygen. Cho Cho began to feel sick. The walls of Lulu's cave began to flake away and die. All the other fish who lived outside in the open ocean couldn't find anything to eat any more. Only Lulu still had some food put by."

But every creature who is born deserves to eat. The bounty of the earth belongs to everyone.

"Lulu placed a big chunk of Cho Cho's divine pink body onto her back. She called out to the other fishes: 'Come and eat the food Cho Cho and I have saved and share it with your neighbors and together we shall swim north to the cool clean waters. Follow me.'"

How many people had suffered to give me my fortunate life? Dad. Mom. Grandma. Grandpa. Maybe it was my job to be fortunate. Maybe it was my job to share my good times and my happy songs and comfort people and get them dancing and help them find their direction.

Follow me.

"You know, if you think about it," I said, "Lucky Boy really belongs to you. I mean, really. You could charge for it." Nikolai laughed. "Don't laugh. Think about it. Lucky Boy is native to your village. You and your cousin Tencing and his family are the only survivors from the village, so according to every regulation governing inheritance, you guys own a share of the land and everything that grows on it. Even with the Chinese Empire taking 85%, you would be rich, like my Uncle Furlong. You'd be a rich farmer."

"But to be that, I would have to live there and work the land," Nikolai said. "And much as I miss my home, I could not live again in any place that is not independent and free. So if there is something to be gained from our family's old purple wheat, it will have to belong to my cousin and his three wives and his 14 children."

I tried to do the math.

"Well then I guess there won't be much profit for them anyway. I mean you can't multiply much seed here in your little greenhouse."

"Multiplying is not the problem," Nikolai said thoughtfully. "Our friend Professor Mugombo has access to other fields, secret floating fields disguised as pleasure palaces, that come complete with willing labor. The difficulty seems to be distribution. Once we have the seed, by what means shall we deliver it to the people?"

"I know how to do that," I said.

"You do?" His teasing eyes. "And how does my Elizabeth know such a thing?"

"Because I have traveled the world and seen many wonders."

I kissed him. Oh, I love to kiss him so much.

There was a soft knock on the door.

"Nikolai. Lizzie. I am sorry to disturb you, but it is time for Lizzie and her ensemble to return to NewLA. Lizzie, please make sure you are packed and ready to depart by three o'clock." We groaned and held each other close. "Ahhh yes yes, well, by all means continue as you were, I suppose five o'clock is time enough."

17. *EMMY made it safely...*

*E*MMY made it safely to the barberry bush on the outskirts of the new city of Xi-an. In her struggle to outrace the murderous fungicidal pellets, she had reached the end of her strength.

Luckily a distant cousin of hers from another branch of her family already resided in the bush. As creatures of the old nature will do, they mated and had some babies. The babies spread through the large, roomy bush, suffusing every stem and leaf and berry.

A cute little black spaniel came racing toward the bush, his ears flying. He didn't pee on the bush like most puppies. He dashed directly into it and tried to hide among its branches. He closed his eyes tightly. His tail stood up straight. His tongue hung loosely, and he panted as though he were still running even though he was now sitting perfectly still.

EMMY's baby burrowed into his fur and all the apertures of his body.

Two Imperial militiamen and an old man with a long white beard crept toward the bush from different sides. They had corn fiber nets with which to capture the puppy. They made no sound. One of the militiamen signaled for all bystanders to back far away from the bush. The bystanders did as they were told.

EMMY's baby flew into the old man's beard. She dusted the shoes of the militiamen and lodged into the cuffs of their pants. She spread herself along the lattice highways of the poised nets.

The old man threw his net first, capturing the puppy, who took a deep breath, erased himself, and exploded, killing his pursuers.

Hundreds of pieces of the bush and the puppy and the men showered Xi'an, carrying EMMY's baby into all the nooks of the new city and the still silent ranks of the surviving terra cotta

177

warriors as well as into other barberry bushes, grown for their maroon beauty as hedgerows separating vegetable gardens.

The death of the old man and the two militiamen was announced on the Chinese Imperial Radiobeam. A moment of silence was decreed for these heroic fallen defenders of the motherland.

Eventually an exchange took place on a small ship in the South China Sea. Collected remnants of Pepper, the puppy SPICEbot, were traded for collected remnants of three goat agrobots, who had smashed up in the mountain gorges of Mongolia, and their brother who had perished in North American custody. The remnants offered no benefit from an espionage point of view, for all the bots were wiped and finished. No, this sad trade was simply a matter of sentiment.

The pieces of Pepper were flown back to North America. After a brief ceremony, Horatio ordered that the pieces should be scattered over the Mohave Spread. All the secret ranks of SPICE joined in his grief.

The fungal spores harbored by Pepper's body floated high on the desert winds and hovered, waiting for spring when they could move north toward the hillside wheat fields.

Hitchhiking on an exchange of spies, EMMY's voracious baby had settled herself on both sides of the Pacific Ocean.

18. LAST NIGHT AT FOXIE'S

The Northern California Agroclans Society meeting almost didn't happen that December because an actual old-fashioned winter snow storm was reported to be blowing in from Alaska. "High winds!   Dangerous whiteouts!" Arliss exclaimed. "Stay out of the hoverlanes!"

Petunia Burton's Incoming buzzed with cancellations.

Then one morning, the voice that came out of Arliss' mouth magically changed. A little girl with a Swedish accent said: "Forget all that snowtalk, shareholders. If anything, expect it to be hotter than usual. Temps in the 70s. Get ready to sweat."

The heartthrob weatherman, who had no idea he had been usurped, continued slogging through drifts, battling the winds, urging his listeners to stay home by a cozy algae fire.

When Arliss found out that he had been the butt of an audio prank, that his audience had been laughing at him without his knowledge, he became enraged and complained to his friend and protector, the Chairman of the Board.

This time, the Chairman refused to heed all diplomatic cautions. He took immediate action.   At a   symposium on monetary policy, in front of the world's leading financial planners, he excoriated the Turkish delegate, declaring that if these sophomoric invasions did not end immediately, the Caliph could expect all out audiowar.

The Turk stood impassive during this attack. Horatio thought it strange that he gave no defense and immediately sent him an invitation to lunch at "Rose'n'Harry's."

After several shots of real Finnish vodka, the Turk said: "Allow me to explain, Horatio. Although it was humiliating to be singled out for derision by your thick-headed Chairman, it would have been more humiliating to admit the truth."

"Define truth."

"We have no idea who is launching these Beam invasions. We cannot find him. Or her. Or them. I assure you we have tried. The janissary corps has shed the blood of the faithful from Berlin to Aswan in the course of our search. Alas, to no avail.

"I could not be expected to admit to such a defeat in a public forum. However, it should have been apparent to any observer, as it was to you although not to your Chairman, that no bone fide agent of the Caliph would waste such extraordinary audio talent on the correction of weather reports and the dissemination of popular music.

"No, Horatio, this Beam thief is a joker. A kibitzer, as my American grandmother used to say. Pan Neutrino. A magic pulse in the earth and a sprite in the fathomless air. Making fools of us all."

Pan Neutrino's mockery of Arliss' broadcast proved correct. That December week turned out to be hot. The farmers canceled their cancellations and showed up in force at the conference.

Most had never attended such an event before. Only a few were old enough to remember free assembly. The very notion of it filled the air with excitement.

The farmers gathered early under a tent set up on the soccer field outside the high school, cautiously getting used to meeting face-to-face with people they only knew virtually. By special arrangement of the Agrotech Division, all their Incomings had been synchronized, and they received the same messages simultaneously. Soil enrichment seminar at ten. Desalination techniques at two by the tennis courts. Snack break at four. They sweated through the sessions, swatted gnats, traded information, argued, gossiped, circulated jokes, admitted their follies, crowed about their successes. It was more fun than anyone could remember.

Petunia directed the Auxiliary ladies to make sure pitchers of cool drinking water always stood close at hand. Her son Odin and the other members of the soccer team guarded every entrance. They wore yellow shirts marked SECURITY, forming a wall of young muscle to guard the proceedings.

The delegates had heard that Horatio Jedda would be attending the final banquet at "Foxie's, Where Dinner Comes a'Singing", with some important news. They assumed it would be an announcement of what they all already knew – the big wheat rust scare had not materialized as a problem for North America.

EMMY had been stopped dead by the agrotechs in China.

The Corporation's expensive EMMY-B-GONE pellets, which the farmers had bought in great fear, were sitting unused on the barn shelf.

The most cynical among them sneered that Jedda had just been trying to create a crisis so the Corporation would increase the Agrotech Division's funding. Others thought Jedda had simply over-reacted because of his inexperience with wheat diseases. They made fun of him, this colorless bureaucrat who had obviously never harvested a field with his own hands. They made fun of EMMY. *Eat your beansies or big red EMMY'll come and getcha!* they said to their kids at snacktime.

Furlong Burton reminded his fellow farmers that one could never know where or when EMMY would next alight. Those fungicidal pellets might be needed next season or the season after.

But "Jedda's Folly" had entered the language of the farmers, threatening to erase "Jedda's Bonanza."

The night before the final banquet, a young orderman broke into "Foxie's, Where Dinner Comes a'Singing." His commanding officer, Major Sally Kim Lee, followed him.

The restaurant was empty, except for a mewing kitten who slipped past Sally's leg, tickling with soft auburn fur. "Well hello there, missus," Sally whispered, scooping up the kitten. "I guess you must be the house mouse control." The kitty licked Sally's cheek with her rough pink tongue and cuddled against Sally's breast. Her collar said GINGER.

"Looks like you made a friend, Major," commented the young orderman.

A trail of moving show biz pictures silently circled the lobby. The sound had ceased automatically at ten PM. But just one look at the fat man dancing, rolling his eyes toward heaven in his admonitions to God, and Sally could not help but hear him singing again, the lyrics forever imprinted in the old song vault of her brain. And then the frog...the mere sight of the skinny green frog brought back the melody of sunny days, no clouds, no ads.

On the stage, a dashing man in a black tuxedo was playing the piano and silently singing. One of those historic interactives so popular with museums now, it had retained a stray shot of energy stored in the sun batteries and just turned itself on.

Sally recalled this performer. He was smooth and suave and sang charming numbers with sophisticated lyrics. He came from the clueless generation, her parents' generation, the do-it-all eat-it-all use-it-all-up generation that Foxie Burton Bright had skewered in her damned song.

People went crazy when Foxie sang that song. They burned their own shacks, attacked the Corporation stores, stole what belonged to others. They hunted down senior citizens and beat them to death. And what happened to Foxie? She seduced the Chairman himself, and while other women, loyal fighting women, were dressed in rags, he showered her with pretty clothes and made her a star.

Sally had seen the pictures that Jedda's spies had filed. Foxie Burton Bright looked just about the same now as she had then. The old whore must've had an awful lot of work done.

"We can't have this Burton Bright woman giving us another generation of recrimination and chaos," Sally had insisted to her superiors in the Orderman Corps. "She's a knee jerk radical, mentoring traitors. She needs to be disappeared. And her blasted granddaughter too. It has been a colossal mistake on Jedda's part to allow the transmission of The Emmy Tour concerts. You can't co-opt these people. You've got to eliminate them completely. Only then will we be able to get on with the business of forgetting the past and have some peace."

The suave singer of charming songs leaned back, shook his head, silently laughed.

"Oh, shut your face, you over-dressed buffoon," Sally snapped.

"Major..." her young assistant cautioned.

However, Sally had already given the signal. The drone bullet, marked with the charge message INSTIGATION TO RIOT, crashed into the singer. He rippled like a dream in water and withered away and then returned, still laughing.

Sally petted and hushed the terrified kitten. The young orderman seemed equally as alarmed. "Just rehearsing," she reassured him. "Familiarize yourself and your unit with the entrances and exits, the hallways, the light grid up top near the ceiling, the hoverstops out back. We'll return tomorrow when all the people are here and the sound is on."

The orderman decided that he'd better mention Sally's overwrought behavior to the Meteorology Department, which was paying him on the side to keep an eye on her.

For the final banquet at "Foxie's, Where Dinner Comes a'Singing", the agroclans came decked out in all the splendor they could muster. These were the blessed and mighty in the Era of Restored Order, but thanks to Horatio's careful philosophy of sufficiency, nowhere near as blessed and mighty as some of them thought they should have been.

The men wore pressed work pants and synthetic leather jackets. The women wore their finest real cloth. Even Evangeline Corelli had dressed up, wrapping herself in a 200-year old lilac silk sari off the rack of antique costumes in her store. Her nice hair hung down. Her scar didn't show.

"The earth moves!" cried her sister-in-law Petunia. "Evangeline is wearing make-up!"

Petunia herself had never looked so beautiful. She wore a dress of rescued gray velvet, and diamonds. Diamonds in her ears and wrapped around her throat, dangling provocatively on the exposed northern slope of her bosom. Smiling envy kissed the air at the sides of her face, saying "Petunia! We heard about your children! How proud you must be!" and complimented her on Athena, soon to return from Antarctica, her professorship at the National University in St. Paul already announced, and Odin just recruited to the gladiators.

Foxie glittered in black sequins. Her mahogany-colored hair glistened under the stage lights. Her eyes, her jewels, her very fingernails glowed.

"You sure look great tonight, Grandma," Odin said.

"You're such a flatterer, my darling. But thank you. I wonder if you could do me a special favor and keep extra careful watch on your cousin Lizzie. A mean southern lady is mad at her about something and has sent her a nasty message with thinly veiled threats."

"We ought to report that."

"Oh, we have. The Agrotech Division people are on the lookout. But it can't hurt for you to help them. Our Lizzie has become a little bit famous. She's an envy magnet now. We don't want any out-of-control jealous rivals stealing her tambourine."

Odin grinned. "Funny thing is, Dad told me to keep extra careful watch on you."

"Me?! Who'd be jealous of a 122-year old restaurantoozy? Don't you worry about me, darling. Watch out for Lizzie. I'll be fine."

Horatio Jedda arrived late. As usual, he dressed badly, spoke softly, met no one's eyes, gestures of nerdiness which few people believed any more. However, he did hold Evangeline Corelli's chair. He did sit next to her. So everybody got the message: Lizzie's EMMY Tour had won the approval of a grateful Corporation. No wonder they were dining at Foxie's.

To Evangeline, Jedda seemed distracted, then suddenly for a moment terribly sad. She pressed his hand under the table in the dark and asked "What is it? What's wrong?"

He gave her a startled, astonished look.

Then he smiled as widely as she had ever seen him smile.

"Nothing is wrong," he said. "In fact, I have had wonderful news."

He was not lying this time.

A SPICEbot named Zaatar, a scorpion stationed at The Sun Project, had been sending messages revealing that the Grain Guardians had found a way to defeat EMMY. They had looked deep into history and disinterred an ancient wheat variety with a natural genetic resistance to the plague. Now they would breed those genes into all the world's wheat, and the people would be saved.

They were keeping their discovery a secret from the Corporation, imagining that they could somehow release it independently, to farmers everywhere, for free.

Horatio had absolutely no intention of impeding their work or telling anybody that he knew about it. If the talent thought they could outwit the Corporation, so be it. Let them enjoy their fantasies. What mattered was that they were destroying the plague.

As soon as their experiments with Lucky Boy proved out, he would commandeer their discovery on behalf of the Corporation and rescue the wheat of the world with it.

By then, if the votes he had put in place stayed loyal, he would have been elected Chairman. The defeat of EMMY would be his first great leadership coup, signature success of the new administration.

He would punish the Grain Guardians with a term of exile at one of the steaming South American plantations. Then maybe, when he retired as Chairman in ten years, he would let them out with a last licks pardon. After all, you couldn't allow the people who had defeated EMMY to rot in the jungle forever.

He thought idly that Zaatar and her entomologist agent would have to get a medal.

That caused him to think of Pepper.

A sharp pang of sadness stabbed.

It was that pang, which Evangeline Corelli noticed, which made her reach for his hand under the table in the dark.

For the first time since Horatio's sliced-off face had been replaced, someone had read its expression.

Surely this was the most wonderful news of all.

The farmers, accustomed to real veggies from their own gardens, didn't enjoy their dinner. But to hear the wait staff warbling charmingly about buttercups and major generals made up for the brightly colored synthetics. When the adorable brother-sister act stood on the balcony up near the lights and sang "Oklahoma", not in a spirited lively way as in the original but slowly, as in a memorial hymn, the farmers cried.

It had cost Foxie dearly to rent that song. She figured it was worth every penny.

She held up her hand for silence.

"We have an important guest with us tonight, and I know you have all been waiting eagerly to greet him. He is Chief Executive Officer of the Agrotech Division. Rumor has it that, despite his youth, he may even be voted in as Chairman of the Board when the current Chairman's term ends in a few weeks. For sure he is the only top Corporation executive who has ever actually shown up in person to speak with us. I give you Dr. Horatio Jedda."

Amid cautious applause, Horatio wound his way among the tables to the stage. He thanked Foxie, greeted the crowd, and to the general surprise, said nothing about EMMY.

"For some years I have been trying to resolve a dispute that has cost our people dearly. I'm pleased to announce that those efforts have finally met with success. We have a new weatherman. He will step in for Arliss..." An angry rumble of protest rose up from the women in the room. "... who has been promoted and will now be coming to many of you every weekday as anchor for a new show called Popular Music at Dawn." The rumble changed to a murmur of approval, with scattered applause and a few happy hoots. "The new weatherman is extremely experienced. He has agreed to train cadres of young weather people in his techniques. Please welcome Eddie Bright."

Eddie strolled off each farmer's Incoming. He sat at their tables, shook their hands. He wore his battered old food drop pilot's jacket. Relaxed and happy, actually smiling, he greeted his public.

"It's good to be back, folks," he said. "Enjoy the warm weather. It will last for five possibly six days. Then a mild form of the old winter will return, with about half an inch of snow." He put his hand on his heart in the gesture that would become his sign-off signature. "I promise to do my best for you. I promise to tell you the truth. This is Eddie Bright the Farmer's Friend. Until next time."

The Incomings went blank. The farmers and their families rose to their feet with a roar of approval.

Odin didn't recognize the fortyish man in the tweed jacket. He couldn't be a farmer. His face and hands were too smooth. And his clothes were too fancy. Shoes made of animal skin. A shirt with wrinkles, like it was woven from actual cotton cloth. And that jacket looked to be real wool, Odin thought, from sheep. The man's Incoming lodged in a bracelet with an unusual shine. He didn't seem to know anybody here. Smiled at everyone but greeted no one. He was moving unhurriedly toward the backstage area.

Odin didn't like the look of him.

The man disappeared behind a pillar.

Odin plowed through a gaggle of giggling farmers' daughters, trying to regain sight of him. The girls wanted Odin to stop and flirt. He extricated himself politely. Looked for the man. Couldn't see him. Too many people.

Then the man reappeared.

He was heading for the dressing rooms.

Odin rushed after him, knocking a fizzy out of the hands of a farmer's wife. The woman yelled in protest, angry about the spreading stain. The stranger turned to see what the commotion was about.

"You! Hold on!" Odin called.

The fizzy lady retorted: "I will not hold on, you rude clumsy boy! This was my dress-up dress!"

The man moved on, into the wings to the right of the stage.

Odin broke away from the lady and ran after him.

In the darkened wings, he tripped over a stack of chairs and went sprawling. He powered his security light. The man was heading toward the dressing rooms where performers prepared and waited to go on. Odin picked himself up and began running.

Lizzie. Where was Lizzie?

The man knocked on the door to a dressing room. He had his hand in his pocket. The door opened. Lizzie smiled in greeting. She was standing among mirrors, wearing some kind of glittering blue outfit. She had blue ribbons in her hair. His geeky bean pole cousin...

God, she's gotten to be gorgeous!

The man's hand came out of his pocket. Odin shouted to warn Lizzie, but his shout was drowned out by applause for an announcement that had just been made out front in the restaurant.

The man took Lizzie's hand and said something that made her smile and then kept going through the dressing room and opened another door. Racing after him, Odin grabbed Lizzie and yanked her into the darkness behind him. "Stay here!"

He charged through the second door.

Paco stopped kissing the man. He turned to peer at Odin. "Hey there, Mr. Gladiator Cousin, what's up? You lookin' for somebody?"

Foxie strode out onto the stage. It was 7:39 in the evening on December 6, 2167. She was, at this moment, the happiest woman in California.

Her son and his wife were wealthy and respected. They had 1600 acres and two successful children. Two healthy children from the same union. Almost nobody in North America had that.

Her daughter looked wonderful for the first time in more than 30 years. The man sitting next to her appeared to admire her, he was pouring her wine, treating her with courtesy, and he was the most important person anybody here had ever met.

The restaurant Foxie had built hummed with excited conversation, racing waiters, the jingle of dishes and glasses toasting the good news. Eddie Bright was returning. Her Eddie. They would be able to live together now, grow old together.

It felt so wonderful, to have good news at last.

The bright stage lights blinded Foxie for a moment. She did not see the ordermen slipping into the back of the hall, quietly dismissing and replacing the security boys. She did not see Major Sally.

"We're not finished with you, folks," Foxie said. "We have yet another surprise to fill the night with joy. As you may know, some of our own kids have actually turned themselves into a pop music sensation. They used to be called Le Tall Band. But recently they changed their name. Let's hear it for The Commons!"

The audience had already begun applauding as the lights came up on the band, which was already playing "Buffalo Girls", which everybody knew since the airing of The EMMY Tour.

Lizzie was wearing a cobalt blue spangled jacket that seemed to pulse with its own rhythm. The ribbons in her hair sparkled and darted like fireflies. The stage lights made her every movement a shower of stars. All the horns and drums that Willy and Sunshine had been gifted with in their travels had rolled on stage. Paco was playing his astonishing smuggled keyboard, producing choruses of people and song birds, the extinct croons of whales and the trumpets of elephants, the galloping hooves of cattle herds and the delicate chirps of gorillas and chipmunks, a vast variegated chorus of the old nature to back up the long array of songs that The Commons sent thundering into the restaurant, songs so old that no rent could be charged, so old that the original way of singing could not be remembered, and the original lyrics and tunes had mutated into new lyrics, new tunes, sort of the same, but different, like the Corporation vegetables, like the Himalayan bears, like EMMY. The majors became minors. The flats became naturals. The slow became rollicking. The wistful became saucy.

It all belonged to the kids now.

The whole audience sang along with Lizzie and her gyrating azure locket and her jangling tambourine.

She reached out to the people.

She sang them a song about a tethered calf and a soaring swallow and the promise of freedom, and soon they were singing along.

She poured herself out to the people with all the love in her heart.

Horatio had never been able to sit through one of Lizzie's concerts. He was a classical man. But tonight, a night of victory, the great plague about to be beaten, his own weatherman in place, his terrible wounds healing at last, he listened attentively.

Evangeline leaned against him, whispering "Oh my baby, my baby…" as her daughter sang. "Isn't she wonderful, my Lizzie? Isn't she just the best?"

"Yes, she is," Horatio answered, for he was a wise man, capable of self-instruction, and he knew that power must shift and grow, that a leader must keep on learning, that times must change.

Maybe, he thought, it starts with the music.

Feeling Lizzie's popularity, her immense influence over the people in the room and the unmistakable political message of her band's new name, Horatio was suddenly struck by a bolt of terror.

A steel fist seemed to close around his heart.

He couldn't breathe.

He realized that he had made a colossal mistake.

He had allowed himself to be blinded by prejudice.

He had critically underestimated the power of a popular entertainer to manipulate events, to steal the attention of the public, to make crowds rumble with anger, murmur with approval, to damage a good name with a well-placed joke, to conjure storms that could limit the attendance at a conference...or a funeral...to enthrall reasonable men and cause them to threaten all-out war and even...ah stupid stupid stupid...even to motivate assassins.

Horatio closed his eyes.

He pressed the back of his left hand against his forehead and sent his thoughts flying.

Esmerelda heard him.

Take Eddie.

Go deep. Right away.

It's Arliss.

Up on stage, Lizzie was asking the audience to quiet down. She had something to say.

"A while back I went on vacation with my Grandma," she said. "It was our family's gift for her 120th birthday. It has turned out to be a very long, eventful vacation. But it has resulted in this evening, and I have my dear Grandma to thank for that. She was in her day a super popular jingle singer. Before then, she would sometimes drop in at a tiny little club in New Jersey and play the piano and sing the songs she loved. So here she is, bringing one of her old favorites back from the past to live with us again. Grandma..."

The tall girl and her band members backed off the stage as Foxie appeared, sitting at the piano, playing the introduction to her song. She looked just the way she had looked when she was young. She was even wearing the same dress.

"End that bitch," Major Sally said.

No one heard the drone bullet coming, because all the members of The Commons, with their magic ears, had gone outside for a breath.

Foxie was waiting for them there with delicious fresh cold water and snacks and hugs and kisses and everything they had always dreamed of hearing. *You were sensational! You're a hit! Everybody loved you! You will be the stars of the 22nd century! Congratulations!*

A suncopter whirred above their heads. Its stairways dropped, spilling the water, scattering the snacks.

Paco's friend was shouting.

"Climb on! Don't argue! Leave the instruments! Just climb on!"

Willy scampered up a stairway. Sunshine grabbed Foxie.

Paco tried to pull Lizzie after him. But by now the uproar from inside the restaurant had reached them. They heard Evangeline screaming.

Lizzie wrenched herself free and raced toward her mother's voice.

Mom was bending over Jedda, pressing a wadded napkin against the spouting fountain in the center of his forehead. His blood and brains and fragments of his skull had spattered her face and her chest. The lilac silk had turned black. I took her in my arms, and his blood got on me too.

She was moaning. "Oh Lizzie, my baby, my beautiful baby girl, look, look, they killed him. He's gone he's gone and we needed him so much. He was the best one he had vision he was ready to change things he was on our side. We finally had a leader, Lizzie. What'll we do now? God, what'll we do?"

Someone threw a hood over my head and tore me away from her. I could feel them prying her fingers off my arms. I could feel my locket being yanked off my neck. I struck out at them and plunged and twisted and choked. It was like I was drowning in the Peaceful Conduct River again.

And all the while, I could hear the interactive of my Grandma Foxie when she was young, vivid as life itself on the stage of her restaurant, playing the piano and sweetly singing:

Many days you have lingered around my cabin door.
Oh, hard times, come again no more...

19. CONSPIRATORS

The Beam carried images of Evangeline Corelli, stupefied with horror, her brother and sister-in-law supporting her, trying to get her out of the restaurant, shouting for people to clear the way.

There were also pictures of Major Sally Kim Lee, wild-eyed, wild-haired, howling in protest as she was being arrested by her own ordermen, that a terrible mistake had been made, the wrong person had been killed, someone must have tampered with the drone code. *Please!* she shouted. *Listen!*

"It has been determined," said Arliss on the weather report, "that the cowardly assassination of Horatio Jedda was ordered by Major Sally, who had lately taken to slandering him in public meetings. It is thought that Major Sally is part of a vast left wing conspiracy involving certain employees of the Agrotech Division already under suspicion of corruption and consorting with competitors."

Among the fugitives was Esmerelda Wolf, Dr. Jedda's longtime colleague, who had betrayed his friendship and organized this horrible plot against him, as well as Dr. Jedda's most trusted scientists, Itamar Mugombo, Felicity Bjornsdottir, and Stevie Foster, turncoats all.

Foster's assistant, Nikolai Juma Das, ("proven beyond any doubt to be a Chinese Imperial agent," Arliss said) was now thought to be hiding out in the impenetrable wasteland of Texas.

The renegade Eddie Bright and his ex-wife Foxie and dozens of others recruited and trained by Mrs. Wolf were part of the vast left wing conspiracy. That included the music group formerly known as Le Tall Band, now self-named The Commons.

"Innocent kids?! Ha!" scoffed Arliss. "First they disrupted a state funeral. Then they caused a riot at The Sun Project. And now we discover that all the while they were in the pay of the Caliph, who has been using their concerts to disrupt Corporation programs for the last two years!"

Members of the vast left wing conspiracy peeled off the cooking show and the sewing show. They accosted the public from walls and sidewalks, stating their names and displaying any distinguishing characteristics which might help in their apprehension.

"These people are traitors," said the Chairman's many voices. "We won't be okay until they've all been brought to justice. Shareholders who assist in their capture will be rewarded with extra energy, water and food."

And so the hunt began.

Two botanists showed up at The Sun Project. They pretended to be experts on oil palms. They spent several days amassing evidence for the show trial that was being prepared in St. Paul. Noting how many young assistants Itamar Mugombo seemed to have, they asserted that he might very well be a dangerous pervert.

They determined that the girls in the greenhouses had previously worked as prostitutes and concluded that the skinny professor had acquired them for his own pleasure. They found a little bedroom at the end of the long hall that was guarded by scorpions. It contained telltale cell residues from various enemies of the state and an incriminating Chinese book.

Ordermen came to arrest Mugombo.

Some pirates got their first.

The pirates killed the two botanists and stole all the workers and all the plants and, sadly for the invading ordermen, set the scorpions free.

Before making his escape, Professor Mugombo transcribed his growing formulae, a pharmacopoeia of precise nutritional processes guaranteed to resurrect scores of plants from the old nature. He entered everything into memory *without* security coding and sent it off to Felicity and Stevie. Then he made copies on paper and instructed his pirate friends to deliver them by hand to hundreds of other prominent plant scientists around the world.

When the ship's captain who took Mugombo to safety asked him why he had shared his great work so freely, he replied: "It's a tradition, Madam. Common scientific practice."

Felicity never received Itamar's communication because her Incoming had been closed down. Her evidence amassers, who had posed as corn and bean librarians respectively, reported that Professor Bjornsdottir often could not remember the names of her closest associates, that she was morbidly obese and so financially reckless that she had permitted the rampant use of protected music without paying rent.

They picked up Athena Burton for questioning. After one long night, she tapped a disc in which she agreed with the investigators that Professor Bjornsdottir should be remanded to the mental institution from which the late Dr. Jedda had so foolishly released her.

Felicity asked the ordermen who were taking her away if she could just go outside for a minute for one last look at the beautiful glacier. It was sunset time and the snow was pink. Being nice guys, they readily agreed.

She thanked them and put on her special lenses so she could see the location of the purple line, and then she stepped across it.

Athena was returned to her family in California. They were all living together now, on three rocky acres, since Furlong's farm and Evangeline's store had been confiscated by executive order of the Chairman.

Athena's hair was mottled with white. Her hands trembled. She was so thin, so gray-skinned, so amazingly *ugly*, that at first, when she tottered off the sunflight, her relatives did not recognize her.

PART FOUR

20. THE NEW DEAD SEA

The ordermen loaded Stevie Foster and Lizzie Corelli into a big, low-flying weather suncopter of the sort normally used for tracking rain clouds and dust storms.

Arliss was there too, but not as a prisoner. From an old-looking bottle, he poured himself a glass of goldish liquor and sipped it with a lot of obvious pleasure, smiling, licking his lips.

Stevie asked him why the Corporation had murdered the head of the Agrotech Division.

Arliss laughed. He said: "Is this really the last question you want to ask in your remaining time on earth?"

"Yeah it is."

Arliss explained that a popular entertainer, with an independent fan base and sole control of the weather report, could control North America. Especially if he had the ear of the Chairman and some money behind him and the nerve not to be merciful.

He had spent his whole life becoming that person, Arliss said. His power was his life's work. And Horatio Jedda was about to take it away from him.

How could Arliss allow that to happen? It was only natural that he should try to defend himself.

And just in case the faceless bureaucrat had some supporters who might feel angry about his elimination, Arliss had seen to it that everybody believed Major Sally Kim Lee had murdered Mr. Jedda.

"Doctor Jedda," Stevie said.

Outside the suncopter window, just north of the picturesque ruins of San Francisco, the New Dead Sea lay gleaming. Lizzie and Stevie reached for each other, realizing that was where they were heading.

"You can't mean to disappear this young girl, Arliss, come on, she's an entertainer, a kid, a talented kid trying to break into show business, once upon a time you must have been just like her…"

"You are wrong, Professor. I was never like big Lizzie here. I was never like anybody but myself." Arliss turned to the ordermen. "Let's get this over with quickly. I'm expected at an important party in North Carolina."

Stevie held Lizzie's hands. His bruised and wounded face was full of anguish.

Nothing seemed more important to her at that moment than to reassure this great man that all his hard work had not been for nothing. So she summoned the voice of her Grandma.

"Not to worry, Dr. Foster," she said. "Lucky Boy is well and strong and he will soon be here."

They flew low over the New Dead Sea.

The ordermen pushed Lizzie and Stevie right up to the hatch of the suncopter as it opened.

A giant bird flew past, carrying nothing in his beak. The suncopter dipped and trembled and almost flipped in the turbulence he created with his huge, fiercely beating wings, unseating Arliss and spilling his whiskey. The eagle turned his noble head to glare at the prisoners.

He looked into Lizzie's eyes.

Lizzie grabbed Stevie Foster's hand and shouted "Jump!"

As I was falling to my death, I had a dream about all the wonders I would never see, which Grandma had been describing to me all my life.

Great coastal cities filled with real food and good times. Skies sparkling with satellites calling out to the universe *We're here! We live here!* Whole countries of tall people towering, the elephants and whales I had only heard on recordings, and meadows brimming with daffodils, and babies, sweet little babies that the elephants and the whales and the daffodils and I would have had if only the kids in Grandma's time had risen up, if only they had gathered together and risen up and demanded a change in the way the world was being used. Oh, it was such a terrific dream.

The dream ended when we hit the water.

We sank down and had to swim hard to retrieve the surface.

It took us a couple of minutes to realize that we didn't automatically float, and we weren't dissolving.

I guess the water must have healed itself finally after so many years, and I guess whoever knew that must have been keeping it a secret and that's what the eagle had been trying to tell me when he looked into my eyes.

I grabbed Dr. Foster and pulled him along with me, because he couldn't swim as well as I could.

We swam south under the shadow of our great leader bird, and eventually we saw a double-hulled canoe with an outrigger and a square sail and a big crew.

Captain Oglethorpe raised his paddle in greeting. And Nikolai reached for us.

21. *Lucky Boy flew on the wings...*

*L*ucky Boy flew on the wings of swallows. They swarmed in black waves over the fields, turning the noon hour dark. They dropped Lucky Boy and his friend, the white violet, in thousands of tiny paper packets, along with little discs that delivered their message immediately upon release from the envelope. And just in case anybody really believed the Corporation's claim that the traitor Lizzie Corelli and her band had been hunted down and disappeared while resisting arrest, the message was sung to the tune of "Miss Betsy from Pike" in the unmistakable sound and style of The Commons.

> **The days will be warm and the ground will be wet,**
> **Just the right combo for EMMY and yet,**
> **If you plant this nursery**
> **Your troubles will end.**
> **A message from Eddie,**
> **The wheat farmer's friend.**

Exhausted from their labors, the swallows flew back to their herders and their new home in the free and independent wasteland of Texas. And there they rested.

California wasn't quite cold enough for Lucky Boy, but he made do. His favorite spots were at the tippy tops of the highest hills, where the wind blew hardest and the sun shone brightest.

Along with the white violet, he was planted in and among the authorized North American varieties. They were big and didn't give him enough room to grow. Their roots squooshed his roots. They hogged all the water and swiped his nitrogen.

He yearned for his old home in the far mountains.

The North American wheat plants started out just great: robust seedlings bound to be a gorgeous golden yellow color. Somebody had tossed a pretty blue necklace into the fields, and one wheat plant grew right through it, looking like a rock star, all decorated and glittering in the sun.

Lucky Boy noticed some weird volunteer plants around the borders of the field. The plants had red spots on their stems. Those spots looked kind of scary.

About two weeks into the growing season, the red spots opened and spread something in the air. The local wheat plants started looking not so great any more. They had tiny flecks of unnatural pallor on their stems.

After another month, the flecks turned into brick red pimples. The big plants kept growing, only they weren't as strong as before. It was like whatever was in the pimples was dragging them down, wasting them from within, making it hard for them to grow flowers and set seed.

The farmers put these sweet-smelling EMMY-B-GONE pellets in the fields to heal the pimples. However, it turned out that the thing that was infecting the wheat wasn't EMMY any more but rather some variety of baby of EMMY, and the pellets didn't do any good.

Since the scientists who had invented the old pellets had been disappeared, their labs shut down, their staff members imprisoned, their agrobots wiped clean, there was nobody left to invent new pellets.

The brick red pimples got bigger and redder, filling up with spores. They stayed put on the big golden wheat for a while. Then they began enlarging, forming oblong clusters of spores that crawled along the wheat stems. The edges of the clusters became ragged and exploded. The spores spilled out, ripping open the tender stems. The fields choked in an ugly orange haze. The golden wheat screamed in agony.

Lucky Boy did not have any brick red pimples.

He felt smashed and buried by the huge sick plants all around him. He leaned this way and that, looking for a little sunshine, but they shaded him and wouldn't let him grow.

Then one night, there was a big storm, with lots of thunder and wind. The big blonde wheat plants, which had once been so strong and proud, blew over like straw, because the red demon had sucked all the stand-up juice from their stems. By morning, millions of plants were lying in the mud.

The farmers crouched in the fields over the dead bodies of their wheat. They looked so sad.

Lucky Boy stood up as straight and tall as he could, smiling in the sunshine, trying to impress the farmers. He was feeling wonderful, getting his share of the good stuff in the soil at last. His spikes were thick with florets. He was setting seed. But he could tell that the farmers were disappointed in the way he looked. They were used to big and bushy and gold, and he was gangly and purple.

All around him the wheat, which by now should have carpeted the northern hillsides, was rotting to its roots, covered by pustules leaking deadly red spores. By harvest time the pustules had turned to gangrenous globules, and the fields resembled a mass grave of tangled black snakes.

From California north to Saskatchewan, not one of the approved wheat varieties survived.

EMMY's hideous baby had murdered the whole harvest.

And Lucky Boy had all the wheat fields for himself.

MAY 2014. BECKET

AUTHOR'S NOTE

The "ancient seer" quoted by Felicity on page 59 is Willa Cather, writing in her 1918 novel, *My Antonia*.

ACKNOWLEDGEMENTS

I am grateful to those many friends who have read and commented on the manuscript at various junctures. They include Stacy Bonos, Sarah Dohle, Philip Lessard, Suzanne Braun Levine, Calvin Qualset, Alan P. Roelfs, Jean Trounstine, Carol Van Why and Richard Zeyen. Special thanks to Melissa Wolff and Karin Lippert for their invaluable assistance, and to Les Szabo for an interview that helped to inspire this book.

To Jenny Stodolsky, loving critic, a prediction for the future: few things are more gratifying than to be well advised by one's own children.

<u>To contact the author:</u>

Facebook:
https://www.facebook.com/susandworkinauthor/

LinkedIn:
www.linkedin.com/in/susandworkin

Email:
readermail@susandworkin.com

Sign up for Susan Dworkin's newsletter to receive periodic updates about her new work as well as her in-person and media appearances:
http://eepurl.com/OuBDr